SAINT MARKUS
UNLEASHED

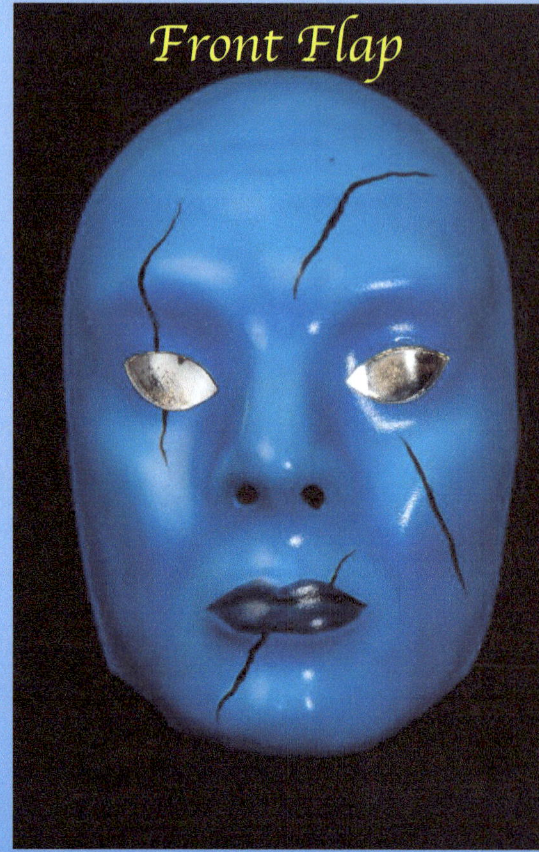

I am going the way of all the earth.
Saint Markus

Saint Markus, a reverent masterpiece, is the most omnipotent, riveting anecdote ever to be released in this age.

It's 98% truth, and 2% fiction.

This apologue, which takes places on a small farm in Mattawamkeag, Maine, is about a family that lived a very unorthodox lifestyle. The Marbellow family reeked in lustful adultery, incest, molestation and homosexual activity. This unadulterated behavior created an infested haven for uncultivated demonic spirits, empowering the most hellacious, antediluvian demon ever to be birthed upon God's given earth.

Morbose, a possessor demon who lurked from Hell, watched the Marbellos, admiring his soon to be Mother and Father's sinful ways years before he was conceived in the sperm of his Father and entered the womb of his Mother. He yearned for the day of his incarnation when he would inherit his earthly name of Markus and his spirit would be embodied by flesh. He also desired the opportunity to exercise the greatest of all powers that he had stolen from the infamous devil himself, Satan.

For stealing The Devil's Bible, Morbose, once Satan's vampiric demon paramour, the most trusted Denali of all servants, is now the most highly sought after nemesis in history.

Dedication

This page is dedicated to my dear Mother, when she passed she left me her words in a hand written tablet, she was writing a book about incest in our big family. I took her words after she died and put them as her wish in this book, many paragraphs and pages of her very own words. This pillow in the photo was hand made for me by my Great Grandmother, my Mother's Grandma before she passed at 97, she knew my favorite colors are yellow and green.

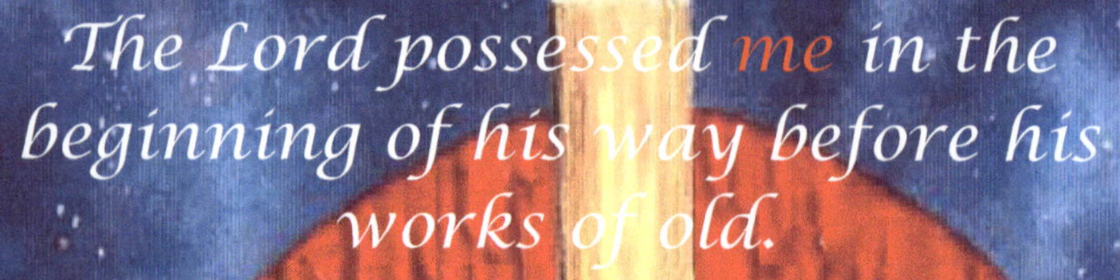

The Lord possessed me in the beginning of his way before his works of old.
Proverbs 8:22

Write the things which thou hast seen, and the things which are, and the things which shall be hereafter;

Revelation 1:19

I was set up from everlasting, from the beginning, or ever the earth was.
Proverbs 8:23
Follow Me: I will lead you to the truths
Saint Markus
Ye Know The Way

Copyright & Publishing

Without limiting the rights under copyright reserved above, no part of this publication may be reproduced, stored in or introduced into a retrieval system or transmitted in any form or by any means (electronic, mechanical, photocopying, recording or otherwise), without the prior written permission of both the copyright owner and the publisher of this book.

The author will prosecute to the fullest extent, which the law will allow. These writs are works of fiction based on a true story. Names, characters, places and incidents have been altered in order to protect the identity and privacy of the individuals involved.

Library of Congress Cataloging-in-Publication Data

Copyright TXu-902-669 The Sexual Vampire / April 12, 1999

Retitled / Copyright TXul-319-981 Unleashed The Devils Bib July 20, 2006

Retitled / Copyright Saint Markus – Unleashed / 2025

Digital book(s) (epub and mobi) produced by Booknook.biz.

Published by: MAM / www.beginning2endpublishing.com

Follow MAM @ www.saintmarkus.info / www.unleashedsaintmarkus.com

Anonymous —Yes　　　　　Pseudonymous — $\mathcal{MAM}$

ACKNOWLEDGEMENTS

I thank GOD, My Mother, Hydie Faith, My Great Grandmother, My friends Flicka, T.J., Kitty Puss, Lil' Gill, Sir Luther, Bentley (AKA) Bunny Rabbets , Cowrinna, Herbinna, Markus, a Lil' J Bird and Carmen. Almonte, my only son.

Oprah Winfrey for her beef story and Martha Stewart for her light blue baby blanket. Costume is anonymous.

The Los Angeles Times, The Mountain Press, The Knox-Journal, Weekly World News, NBC Today Show and many more.

Bonnie, Danny, Midnight Rose, Belinda, Melissa Tweedy, H. W. Longfellow, The Bishop, Bob Hastings, The wonderful Gold Coast Bar, The Golden Bull Restaurant and Arthur. Porky, Magpie, Buffy, Mother Love, 420-B.P., The Barn-Fairy, Chief Love Heart, Hatchet Ass, Sassa, H.H.&H.H., MAM and then SER. My EX- ED along with Tommytoes, Lips, Injun Howling Breeze, Mr. Rogers, Jory, Ashley, Lola, Cucu Ielaki, Garden Lady, Marshall, Si, Rick, Serbian Lady of all hearts, Ani, Aaron, Megan & Hannibal.

Oh yes, the best thank you ever goes to all the most wonderful, fantastic Face Book friends and followers. I adore every one of you. Saint Markus was re-done for you and is yours forever and ever.

A very special thanks to Lady Marguerite and Sir Edward. Their unique harmony has created a one-of-a-kind ART-WORK for the reader and the Vampires intimacy unto each other; indubitably a pleasure.

The Holy Bible
The Devils Bible
Last, but not at all least, YOU, the reader, I adore.

THANK YOU

*If one peeled away 666:
Under those numbers is GOD:
For He hath created All:
Which leaves Him:
Not under: Yet above:*

I've lived the human life for 50 years.
Markus

PROLOGUE - SEPTEMBER 1998

At a funeral home in a small town in Missouri, a family congregates for services. This is undeniably a screwed-up bunch of people. Of the thirteen original family members, only two have been able to sustain stable relationships. Their trails are littered with infidelities, failed marriages, countless car crashes and a death. As of four days ago, two deaths. Even today, on this special day of remembrance, most of them are mad at each other and not speaking.

Automobile wheels spin down a paved highway toward the funeral home. Those smoking outside on the steps see a small dot, which becomes an approaching black limousine. Two attractive women—one tall, crop-haired and mannish in a pantsuit and the other, shorter with curls, wearing a black little-girl dress—turn to each other and say at the same time, "Oh, my God!"

The loud man in jeans and boots talking to a soft-spoken businessman in a sharp suit says, "*Day*-um!"

The long car pulls up front, and a disapproving chauffeur opens the rear door. The smells of marijuana, expensive perfume and vomit waft out, in that order.

A pointed toe in black patent leather, a stiletto heel and a shapely leg in black fishnet slide out. An elegant woman emerges, veiled and dressed in black from head to toe. Mouths drop open and all eyes are on her, fascinated. Clearly, the family has no idea who this is.

"This is just like in the movies!" Hydie whispers to her husband Dube.

The woman's feet are unsteady and at one point, she scrapes her heel on the sidewalk. Practically gouges a trench, actually.

For the lips of a strange woman drop as an honeycomb, and her mouth is smoother than oil: But her end is bitter as wormwood, sharp as a two edged sword. Her feet go down to death; her steps take hold on hell.

Proverbs 5:3-5

Inside the funeral parlor, her gloved hand signs the guest register:

M.A.M.

TABLE OF CONTENTS

SAINT MARKUS

There are a few places toward the end of the book where one might want to use a looking glass!

May things be more clear......

By

M.A.M

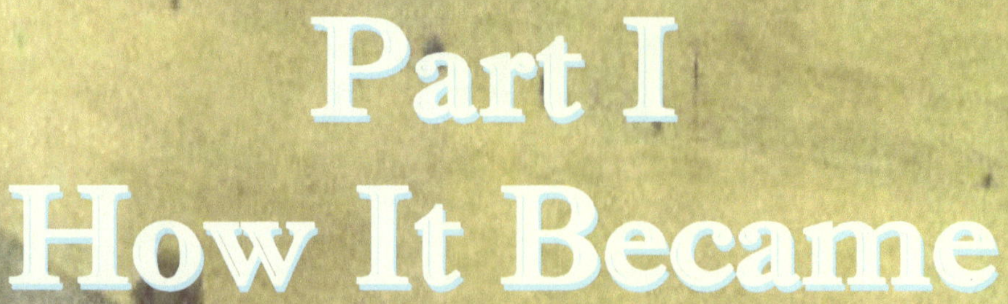

Part I
How It Became

Is not the whole land before thee? Separate thyself, I pray thee, from me: if thou wilt take the left hand, then I will go to the right; or if thou depart to the right hand, then I will go to the left.

Genesis 13:9

Many Truths in Many Places

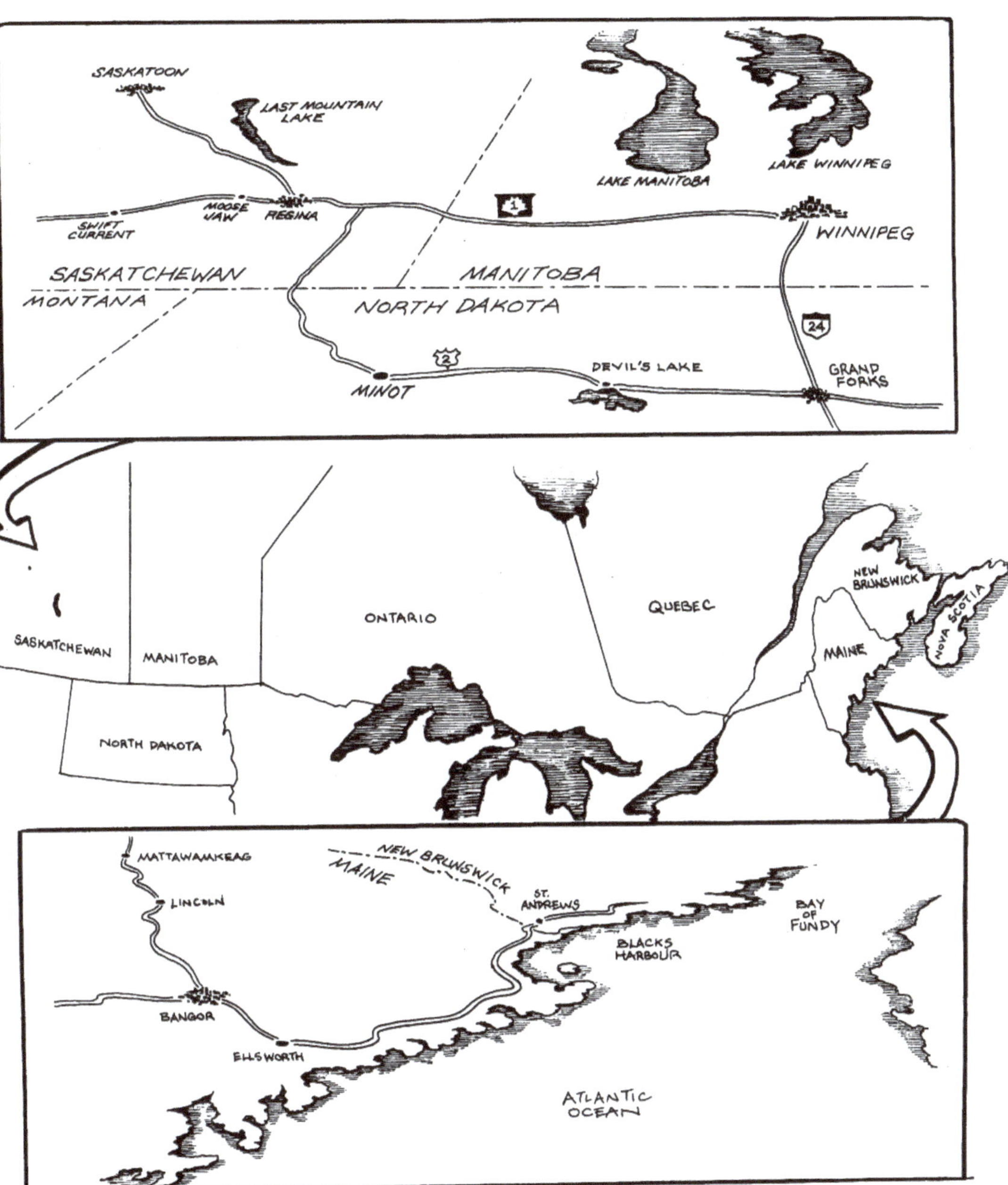

Chapter 1

Demonism

I want to tell you how I evolved, how I came to your Mother Earth. I am a demon straight from Hell and my name is Morbose, which is pronounced Mor'ba sigh.

Not so long ago, I made my first visit to your precious earth. I have never left and never will.

I am diurnal as well as nocturnal, of the day and of the night

I came in the form of a demon—the kind that you cannot see, only feel. Demons cannot gain any power by being on their own; they need a host of sorts, a body to overtake. They have to feed on your soul to become more powerful.

I want you to know that I was feeding on my father's soul before he even became my father, it truly was unreal, but it was my only chance. You see, being a demon wasn't enough for me. It's unfulfilling, like being inside a black, angry, cold space. I didn't want to be in anyone else's body, either. I wanted a body of my own. I wanted to create myself: a demon in human vampire form.

Human vampire form is the most powerful form that any demon can ever hope to achieve. It allows the demon to intertwine itself into human life and society. A living, breathing demon, inside of a human shell . . . Can you think of someone or something that is any less obvious? I didn't think so, that's why it works. Ha ha ha!

Many times, have you not had a chill go up your spine or felt a cold spot in a room? This normally indicates that a demon is very close. If it wants to stay, then you will have a hard time getting rid of it. Night after night, it will try to force its own evil soul and shadowy form into your body.

If you have ever all of a sudden sat straight up in bed, then there was a demon trying to get into your body. Yes, the demon could force its way into your body during the day, but if you knew about it, you would probably commit suicide. That's why it chooses to bump out your soul, while you're in the deepest part of your sleep, totally taking over your body with you, in the dark, not knowing this, not knowing what is happening or what is going on. Where else is your soul going to go, but back into your own body, where the demon now has full possession.

These kinds of demons, which are among the many sent out of Hell to do the Devil's bidding, are called the Possessors. I am one of these. We are solid, but a human being can only sense us by way of cold spots, bad odors or the feeling that someone is watching them. We can read human minds and know when you are most vulnerable.

People are not meant to see or touch demons, for that's the way God intended it to be. On the very rare occasion, humans have caught glimpses of us. Most of the time though, they do not. For we are silent killers.

I will take you into a world that I have already lived. And show you the darker side of the world that you call your own.

Morbose. The Morbid One. This is how am I known in my world.

Markus Antoney Marbello is how I will be known in yours.

Since vampires are derived from demons, I will always carry the demon within me, no matter how human I may appear.

We are going in and through what is behind me now. The only way to get the truths to you is for me to write this and put it in book form, for you have a right to know them.

Giving heed to seducing spirits, and doctrines of devils.
I Timothy 4:1

It has been almost two thousand years since you tortured and killed Christ. I am an adult demon, highly evolved for my kind. I want to be highly evolved among humans, too. I am determined to be the first living vampire of this kind. I have a plan for a certain family, working it out meticulously to culminate in 1963.

But everything is backwards: RETLEKS RETLEH

As it turns out, I will be helped by something I don't even believe in. Luck. For until now, I did not think it existed.

My plan was to be born as a human child. I'd decided to be raised as a farm boy in Maine until I could achieve my independence. Wanting, as I did, to possess a living, breathing, blood-pumping entity—a human—to become a vampire, I reasoned it would, of course, be less detectable in a large farm family, because everyone was so active. There were some things though, that even I did not expect.

Long before I possessed my father's body, I had studied this family. I watched and I waited seven years until the time was right for this to happen. This family had a lot going on; busy parents, many unsupervised kids, lots of animals, a location far out in the country. *Far out,* turned out to be the operative term here.

Bill Marbello, the man I had chosen for my father, was of medium height and average build. He had dark coloring and glasses on a beaked nose under a bald head. He moved quickly and had a loud, deep voice, bear-like and growly. On the farm, he wore work clothes, but never overalls. He didn't like animals. They were just business to him. A hard worker, strict taskmaster, boisterous, carefree, this man played favorites with his kids and didn't care if the others saw or not. He was a genius at driving wedges between people with his lies.

Out of town most of the time and home only on weekends, he lived a promiscuous life. Long before he met me, he was begging for evil to come into his life. You could tell by his actions. He was weak-willed and had a bad temper, which exploded quite often. His mind was a lustful one, full of perverted thoughts and sinful kinks. Bill knew the wrong things he did, but he never expected to be possessed by such soul-devouring evil.

When I went to him, he was more than ready.

Marian Marbello, my future mother, was a beauty in her younger years with big, brown eyes and fluffy, dark, brown hair. She was soft-spoken, short and now, wide-hipped and plumpish after bearing children. She had long nails on one hand and short ones on the other for the artificial breeding of cows. She was sincerely religious and a prankster who had fun with her children. Marian was blinded by love and whisked away by life. Once her husband had "the wife" in place, working on the farm and producing babies on a regular schedule, he felt free to go his merry, feckless way.

I'll let her speak for herself in a moment in her own words. I've reproduced her handwriting as closely as possible and I have not changed anything, not a single word, even her spelling is the same. She'll tell you plenty. I did have to correct if a word was spelled wrong.

The night that I planned to possess Daddy's body was also my first night on earth and truly, I had waited a long time. The family I'd been watching so carefully lived outside the small rural town of Mattawamkeag, Maine in a two-story farmhouse with an attic and a basement. It was foggy and misty. You couldn't see a thing. The fog hung low, stuck to the ground.

Although I could not see, it didn't stop me in any way. My hunger, my very existence depended on *possessing* this evil soul. I could feel the beating of his distant heart in my chest so strongly it felt like my own. I could hear what he heard—the sounds of his family feeding themselves silently. He was making their mother stand over the children with a whip tonight. They had to raise their hands to speak. God forbid; anyone should enjoy themselves when my father was angry.

Usually, my mother was in the next room, smoking a cigarette alone by the fireplace, while the others ate. If anyone came in, she'd sling the cigarette into the fire and pretend that she hadn't been smoking, but it was an open secret. She never once sat down and ate with her family.

The closer I got, the more anxious I became. I reeked.

Demons have a very powerful and putrid smell to them. They smell even worse when they are weak, because they are dying, again and again, until they find a host.

Every creature fled at my approach, some noisily, as they sensed my black, raging energy plunge forward. At this point, I only concentrated on one thing, it didn't matter what happened. I just wanted to *get there.* Saliva and foam ran out of my preternatural mouth as I lunged along a steep mountain chain called the Appalachians. My new home in Maine lays ahead. I went by way of the forest, so the chance of being detected by farmyard dogs was kept to a minimum. I seethed through the forest, a dark, shadowy thing, breaking branches and snapping limbs. All I could think of was getting to his body. I didn't want to roam the earth in search of an unwary soul. It would wear down my energy. I had it all planned, it was crucial for me to get there that night.

I knew that I was almost at the house, because my breathing started to quicken. It felt as if *his* heart was in my throat. The pounding in my head made it feel like it was going to burst. But, through all this, I could sense that something was wrong.

Oh, yes, something was very wrong.

Something as evil as I awaited me at that house in the night. What was I picking up on? I had not foreseen this. I hate it when my plans are messed up. I don't adjust well.

Anger and worry consumed me.

I could barely see the house from where I was. There were huge, red, cedar, black walnut and white, pine trees in my way. I knew no one could see me, but I wanted, nevertheless, to be very careful. Dogs are especially sensitive to something evil. They can smell the characteristic stench that evil produces and their hearing is very keen. The last thing this situation needed was a bunch of dogs barking their heads off.

Ever so slowly, moving as quietly as I could, I edged my way past tall, blueberry bushes to the side of the house and toward a basement window. It was almost impossible for me to keep my breathing low. I had been waiting for this for far too long.

The basement window was locked from the inside. I extended my huge, right, indistinct arm and pushed steadily. By putting slow pressure on it, I made the four screws on the latch quietly give way. It was best for me to stay down there, at least for one more night. It was about five-thirty in the morning, and I didn't have enough time, not if I was going to do this in the dark.

The basement was huge, a demon's den. It had a thick, old, wooden window to throw potatoes down into a plywood bin for winter. There were all kinds of canned goods along one whole wall and a big, wood-burning, iron furnace on the other side of the room. Behind, it was the plank steps that led upstairs. I went up to the door at the top. The steps didn't have backs to them, nor was there a railing. It was damp and musty-smelling, and I could hear water dripping from one of the corners.

I tried to figure out what I'd sensed earlier, what was amiss in this house. I stepped out into the big kitchen, making it smell like rotting food.

The "thump, thump, thump" of a child bouncing down the stairs from an upstairs bedroom made me pause. It was four-year-old Jerrod, with an unwelcome surprise. Lobo, an eerie looking dog with weird, blue eyes, was with him. The white German shepherd usually slept in the tool shed which was attached to the calf barn.

Two seconds after sensing them, I was back through the door and on the basement steps, waiting as I listened for them to pass. Jerrod came around in a few minutes, mumbling to Lobo, who was whining. If only the child knew what, or rather who, Lobo was smelling.

After I was sure that Lobo and Jerrod were gone, I headed back up the stairs, thinking of my plan and also of getting a better look at the inside of the house. All I wanted was to possess Daddy's body and through his semen, transfer into my mother to create myself as a living vampire.

My dear sweet mother, she was prolific as hell and never had a problem getting pregnant. Her first four kids were eleven months apart; the oldest girl was seven and her brothers were six, five and four. Mom would have eleven children and two miscarriages with one still born before she was through. And I would be one of them.

For now, Mom was six months along, with a baby boy. This would allow me to possess and feed off my father's soul, which was very powerful and rich nourishment for a demon, until the baby was born and another life was conceived. This bit of time would give me enough power to transceive into my mother's womb.

I returned to the basement with my plan firmly set in my mind.

*   *   *

MARIAN'S VADE MECUM
(Personal Hand-Writings)

In 1997, a year before she would die of cancer in Stockton, Missouri, Marian Marbello lit a generic cigarette and tried to decide what to call her book. She wanted to write the story of her life. She looked around the trashy trailer that she and Weasel her new love shared and saw the God-awful place for what it was, but she didn't care. She couldn't. Severe, untreated depression over the years had changed her and she had nobody close who understood how ill she was.

She didn't know why she was like she was, why the toilets were falling through the floors, or why mud dauber nests dotted the living room ceiling. Her children were baffled as well. Was it a rogue character flaw, which somehow showed up in the second half of her life? Sadly, no it wasn't. . . a sick animal fouls its own nest.

On the porch was an oven door that she'd pulled out of the stove and was using for a cat box. It was overflowing with nauseous kitten poop and sick kittens. They had mucous eyes and distended bellies.

Her kids didn't let her grandchildren visit her, because they'd come away with scabies, a parasitic, skin mite.

When it rained, the river of water under the trailer was twice as wide as her sofa. It was raining right now, a flat, gray rain with no sparkle. In fact, everything looked flat and gray to her. There was no color in her life anymore. The window in front of her reflected her sad face, once so pretty. Her life was right there in that view; a cemented hole in the ground with logs lying around, wet and rotten. The beginnings of her dream home that would never be built.

What a life, she thought. Eleven kids, two miscarriages, one still born, a divorce and now, this breast tumor business.

She had wanted a big family. She got a big mess.

She picked up a pencil, so she could erase her mistakes. Pity she couldn't erase Bill as easily.

Ironically, Marian never once erased anything, as she unerringly told the truth, from beginning to end. She wasted neither space nor words, nor time complaining. It was what it was. She couldn't care any more. On page one, line one, she wrote her first of many Vade Mecums, meaning personal handwritings.

This all began in Sept. 1953, when I met a wonderful man. He was 10 years older than myself. We met at Church.

He was living with a wonderful Christian couple. We dated, he was easy to talk too. But I wasn't much of a talker. But he made up for it, he could talk you in and out of something in the same sentence.

It took 9 months plus 2 weeks and we were married on June 29, 1954. I than became Mrs. William Marbello. I had just turned 17 the 16th of June. Bill was the love of my life. I had him on a pedestal. To me he could do no wrong. He was the boss all the way. We had our share of fights, and also had the fun of making up. Our love life was wonderful. (Or so I thought.) On Feb. 4, 1955, we had a beautiful baby Girl. We named her Jacqueline, Jackie for short. She was our pride and joy.

*   *   *

Morning dawned on June 1, 1962. And in just a little while, everyone was awake and running around. They acted like a bunch of wild animals. There were four kids on the ground and one inside my target mother Marian, whom I shall call Mom. And, of course, Bill . . . Daddy.

The school bus picked up the kids and Mom left the house to go shopping. I could hear the tractor running, so I assumed Daddy was outside. I detected a noise on the other side of the basement door. It was that bastard dog Lobo. He could sense my core-rotting, evil stench. He started whimpering and carrying on, scratching the door and even barking a little. *Not very bright, Lobo, old boy.*

I swung the door open. He got a look at my true form and froze. I kicked him hard, one time. He ran like a scared bunny through the kitchen, wailing the whole time, and then, out the back door, he went.

I went upstairs where everyone, except for the newborn children, slept. I found a door at the end of an upside-down, horseshoe-shaped hallway. The door and knob on it were smaller than regular size. It was to the left, somewhat back in a corner, just past Mom and Daddy's room. I opened it and a stairwell curved upward and to the right, mysterious and quaint. I was charmed—this was going to be perfect. I was now, in the attic, right over their bedroom and it wouldn't be long before all the chores were done, and night fell.

Yes, I was going to enjoy life on Earth or so I thought.

Time passed slowly, but finally Mom returned from her shopping and the kids were all home from school. The cows were milked, the calves and hogs fed, the milk barn washed down, and the garden watered. Supper was served and cleaned up. All homework was finished and prayers said. Finally, everyone was tucked in, snug as could be.

Now all I had to do was wait just a few more hours, until the household was in its deepest slumber. It didn't seem long at all before I heard some faint noise, but as quickly as I heard it, it was gone again. I moved over to open the window—the time was getting nearer. I slid out onto the porch roof, so I could look in all the windows. I went around to the right, to look in Daddy's window and he was not to be seen. Only my mother lying there, sleeping. I was instantly outraged, because one of the best times to take over someone's body is when they are dreaming and he wasn't there.

Of course, I would find him. If I did not possess him this night, then I was willing to bump him in the daylight, if I had to, despite the risk to him.

I went around to the other side of the porch, where the kids' bedrooms were. If he was not up in them anywhere, then I would go down into the house and search it from attic to basement.

The first window was the spare room. It was for the latest hired hand. The second window was Jackie's, my future, oldest sister. The third window belonged to Matthew, Jason and Jerrod. When Jake was born, it would become his room as well.

I moved on past the spare room and up to Jackie's window, peeping just a little around the frame. She was a petite, pretty, giggly blonde, with her mother's big, brown, doe eyes and crooked teeth. As she got older every adult around her wanted a piece of her . . . .

I could see a man on the bed with her. He had one hand up between her legs and with his other hand, he was manipulating himself. Jackie moaned as she threw her head back to escape her guilt at looking into this man's eyes. I'd moved to the center of the window to get a better look when the man turned and looked straight into my eyes.

It was Daddy and his eyes had a slight, greenish glow to them.

*　　*　　*

MARIAN'S VADE MECUM

She'd found a new steno pad in the trailer Weasel had just put in her name. He shared it with her, when he wasn't in Michigan with his wife and daughter. Marian hated sharing Weasel. It just wasn't her way. However, there was nothing she could do about it and she loved him. Weasel was good to her. Meagan, her youngest, must have bought the pad for school and never used it before she dropped out to get married.

Before Marian found this steno, she had already written a list of eight possible titles on a smaller piece of notepaper and now, she taped it inside the cover. She reviewed it. She'd neatly numbered nine lines down, but the ninth one was blank. Eight phrases said it all:

<u>Book Name</u>
1. Things You Just Don't Know
2. How Bad Can it Be?
3. Married Bliss -vs- Living Hell
4. Marriage Gone Bad
5. How Incest makes you feel.
6. Incest In Lg family
7. <u>My life with Incest</u> *
8. A family Broke apart

Her family . . . Lord Jesus . . . her kids . . . .

Alone, in a trailer in the middle of the state of Missouri . . . Misery . . . Marian put down her pencil, so she wouldn't poke her eye out while she sobbed. When she was finished crying, she picked it up again.

Jackie had a girlfriend named Sherry. About this time Sherry came to me, and said that one night when Jackie spent the night she had told her that her Dad had molested her. I told Sherry not to ever say anything like this again about my husband. And that I didn't want to hear it. I loved Bill enough to still believe in him. He always called me at 10pm every night. Sherry came back and told me again about Bill molesting Jackie. Again I told her not to talk about Bill that way, and to get out and don't ever come back.

* * *

Although a demon can protect itself from another demon reading its minds, their presence in a human or animal is detectable by an unnatural glow in the creature's eyes. The color of the glow, like a human's unique fingerprint, usually identifies the demon. Rashma, a demon of chaos who was vengeful, immature, and had no self-restraint at all, already possessed

Daddy. It was his poisonous presence, like a stinking, public bathroom at a beach, overflowing with refuse and contamination, that I had sensed before even reaching the house.

I fumed. This wasn't supposed to have happened. How could Rashma have messed up my plans like that? I presumed that body was *mine*. Rashma had cheated and stolen Daddy from me.

Daddy finished his evilness and went back to bed while I tried to think about what to do now that I knew about Rashma. Maybe Rashma thought I was just passing by, but surely, he must know who I am. Has he not heard of *Morbose?* I could crush that body he was in as well as him with little effort, but I would not do that—I needed my father for my ultimate plan, and I refused to change it. I had selected my daddy carefully and didn't want to create such a fight inside of him that he ran off the edge of a cliff. But then getting and staying inside of a body with another demon is a very risky proposition.

Although . . . If mastered properly, one could feed even on a demon's soul, but that would only work if Rashma had far less power than I.

I had been doing my homework and wanted to become more than Rashma ever could be as a demon. I wanted to go into the next world, to live my dreams as a vampire, and he was not going to stop me.

Daylight was setting in and I knew it would be but a short wait, until night fell again. What I did not know was that Rashma had also been doing his homework.

*　*　*

MARIAN'S VADE MECUM

When I met Bill I was 16 years old. I was still a virgin. Bill was the only man I had ever had.

Which we did go all the way before we got married. I was 1 month P.G. when we got married. I am not ashamed of it, because I loved him very much.

After Jackie was born we bought a old run down house by my folks. He fixed it up and sold it, so we could buy a farm. I always loved kids, horses, dogs, cats and all animals. We started out with hogs on our farm. We had a baby boy March 4, 1956. Matthew was born on our farm. Bill was the type if he had a dollar in his pocket, he would spend $2.00. Bill couldn't make a living with the milk cows that we now had, so he went back to work on the road in construction and hired a boy to milk the cows. The hired men came and went. I never had any interest in any of them. I only had eyes for my man Bill.

*   *   *

Nighttime fell again and all the evening chores were done, the kids were getting tucked in by Daddy. Mom had gone to bed a little early, exhausted from working too hard, this far along into her pregnancy.

Every night, Daddy would go to each room and say prayers with the kids. I couldn't understand him doing that, then turning around and doing what he was about to do, and made a habit of doing it, indiscriminately and often.

After prayers, he climbed into bed with Mom, snuggling up to her and breathing slowly, but he was only pretending to go to sleep. He lay there, fully awake, waiting, just like me, until the time was right.

I came down from the attic and slipped into the hired hand's room. I needed to be there before Daddy, just in case Rashma tried to object and I had to demonstrate a few home truths to him.

It wasn't long before Daddy got out of bed, naked, careful not to disturb Mom. He loved to walk around at night naked. From the beginning, he'd made it plain to Mom that he did not like houseguests for this very reason. He went to the bathroom at the top of the stairs, right in the middle of all the bedrooms. He relieved himself quickly and went on to the room where the new hired hand slept.

Daddy sure was lecherous and Rashma's sexual gluttony merely fueled fires that were already burning.

Joe, the farmhand, heard Daddy go to the bathroom and was waiting. He had grown up on a poor farm in the boonies of Illinois and aimlessly hired himself out, here and there. He liked it in this new place just fine. He didn't mind watching the kids as part of his duties. . . And he sure liked Daddy.

From the way Daddy stared at his crotch when he hired him, Joe knew what was up. Fine with him. Daddy's bulge had looked good when he returned "The Look" and, like most men, he was ready for some action, whenever and wherever, from anyone.

As soon as Daddy came in, I knew Rashma wanted me to join them. It figured. His appetites were out of control. I'd go with it, use it as a hidden tool. His lust was my gain.

Rashma wasn't thinking properly. He was too epicurean, like a crazed beast. *How can he be so careless with me?* I wondered as I watched them closely.

Right then, Rashma turned to me and let me know, without speaking a word, that if I wanted my father's body, I could have it very soon. He willed me to come forth. I could feel this in all of my being and gathered myself to spring.

Rashma had Joe submitting to all of his needs and Joe was really getting into it. I think he was falling in love with Daddy. They were fornicating, my father on top, his back to me. Then, Rashma turned my father's head to me, so that I could see the faint, green glow of his demon eyes.

Now, Morbose! Now!

I jumped with all my force. I didn't want to cause too much of a scene, but damn them to Hell, I had to get in. I had to make it. I wanted it for my life, my whole being, my very existence. I bumped Daddy pretty hard, for I wanted to more than insure my new property and knocked him completely off and to the other side of Joe's tight, smooth body. At the same moment that I hit my father's body; he started to have an orgasm.

Feeling a bit disoriented, Daddy picked himself up and mumbled, "I'm tired, going' back to ma'room."

That night, I got to lie beside my mother, before she became my mother.

Now, I had to deal with Rashma. Why did he want me so desperately? Why did he issue such an unresisting invitation? *Two very good questions.*

I could feel Rashma in my father's body with me. He was staying down in the lower part, just waiting. I didn't feel negative power from him or bad vibes in any way; although he must have known that the upper body has full power. I just thought that I would have felt him more.

I could have thrown Rashma out, but if he didn't want to leave, then there would be a fight that could put my father's life in jeopardy. Curse him, if he started something like that. If he tried to bump me, I would crush him instantly, for I was in command now, no matter what his intentions were. I wasn't about to put my destiny into the hands of some little piece of demon-crap that had pre-empted me. If things stayed like they were right then, maybe I would let him be, for he knew that if I didn't get what I wanted, then he wouldn't get what he wanted either, whatever that was. For Rashma to have called out my name the way he did, proved that he knew who I was. Maybe that's why he was so still; he knew how strong-willed, demonstrative and powerful Morbose really was. Possibly, he wasn't as stupid as I thought.

*   *   *

MARIAN'S VADE MECUM

We had another Boy, Jason, July 2, 1957. Bill spoiled this boy something awful and he always had to compete against his older brother.

We always wanted a lot of children so in June 1958 Jerrod was born the day after my birthday on the 17th. After Jerrod was born I started smoking, which Bill didn't want me to do. But I had gained a lot of weight, and I thought it would help me keep my weight down. But it didn't, now I just have a bad habit. Now I wish I had never started. Bill smokes and chews, It was okay for him, but not me.

In July 1962 we had another boy Jake. This made four boys.

*   *   *

It was now around the First of July 1962.

The weather was nice, and farmers were cutting their pastures to make hay. Most of the baby birds were fully-grown and singing in the fragrant air. The little foals were well on their way and everything was blooming with life - including Mom. She didn't have very long time to wait for the new baby. It was only a matter of days. She could hardly get around and spent most of her time in bed. Summer is rough on a pregnant woman and Mom worked way too hard, even with the baby due so soon. Daddy just stood by and let her half kill herself, although he wouldn't allow her to do much else.

The screen door slammed open, and somebody boomed, "Anybody home? Hey, Marian, I'm here!"

Mom's baby sister, Aunt Linda, had arrived on the scene.

This was Aunt Linda's first time helping with the kids and the farm while Mom was having a baby, for Mom had too much pride to ask the same woman to help her every time.

I call her Aunt Linda, but it's with no pleasure, as you will see. She was a tall, sturdy woman, with broad shoulders, small hips, big hands and a deep voice. Blunt, bossy, very loud, and unethical (she wore pantsuits to the local Baptist church), she was funny and boisterous in a room full of people. Daddy and her were two of a kind: backstabbing, conniving, cold and quick toward most of the boys, but partial to Jackie.

To her credit, though, Aunt Linda was a big help and always there for my mother when she needed her. She was also kind of cool in her own way. When any of the kids cut school, they could go to her house, hang out and she'd serve Kool-Aid. Given her normal attitude toward kids, though, I think her motivation for doing that was to keep Daddy close to her.

Joe and Daddy were busy in the fields. There was much work to be done during this time of the year. They had to store up feed in the summer for the cows during the winter. They spent the biggest part of the day cutting and chopping the forty-four acres of young corn. Once they brought it up to the barn area, it was blown up into the silo, where it fermented into silage and developed a sweet-sour smell to it. The cows just went crazy over this stuff.

Daddy let Joe finish while he came in to work on the cycle mower machine, so he could start the first cutting of alfalfa, early in the morning. Plus, he wanted to check on Mom and that was fortuitous, for right about the time he walked into the house, she started having labor pains.

"Bill . . . "

Her hospital bags had been ready for three weeks, waiting for this moment. Aunt Linda and Jackie helped Mom to the car, while Daddy retrieved her things and put them in the trunk. Matthew, Jason and Jerrod just stood there, with their mouths hanging open, as if they were in shock or something. Aunt Linda rounded up the kids and shooed them inside.

"Come on, come on, everything's going to be just hunky-dory. Don't you worry about it," she assured everybody within ten miles. "Let's go have some pop."

Daddy sped off toward Bangor and the county hospital, his first choice, as if he didn't think Mom could make the decision for herself. About halfway down Interstate 95, he almost hit a moose that had come up out of the Penobscot River, which ran a very close parallel to the interstate in this area. He came about two inches from sending them both headlong through the windshield at sixty-five miles an hour.

My mother grabbed her stomach and bent in agony as another labor pain set in and her water sack broke all over the seat. If only she could hold on just a few more minutes . . . *Darn,* she thought, *I meant to tell Jackie to bring that towel.*

"I'm sorry about getting the seat all wet," she sobbed, fearful of his reaction.

"Don't worry about it. Just breathe…IT'LL be just fine."

When they arrived at the emergency room, Daddy ran in to let the nurses know. By the time he ran back out with help, Mom was almost out of the car.

*   *   *

MARIAN'S VADE MECUM

When he was out of town and called home, he would talk to me for about 10 minutes and swear around 30 to 40 times. Instead of saying how are you. He would say how in the hell are you. He was always swearing. And I always didn't like it.

Bill was never their when any of the children were born after the 1st one.

*   *   *

Not that which goeth into the mouth defileth a man;
but that which cometh out of the mouth, this defileth a
man.
St. Matthew 15:11

"Dammit, Marian, why in hell didn't you wait, like I damn well told you to?" Daddy griped, helping her up the sidewalk and into the building. The nurses took over from there. They helped Mom onto a gurney and rolled her away. My father went on to the nurses' station and checked her in. When he was finished, instead of waiting around for even a little while, he went straight out to the car and drove home.

By the time Daddy got back to the farm, Mom had an eight-and-a-half pound bouncing baby boy, and he didn't even care enough to call. His thoughts were totally consumed by Aunt Linda as he drove home and pulled up to the house, cutting the lights and shutting off the engine.

Aunt Linda was the goal, the next conquest. Rashma was stirring. I could feel him. He was a part of this, as was the demon within Aunt Linda.

She and Daddy went upstairs to his and Mom's bed. Soon, Aunt Linda would get more than she ever bargained for.

Chapter 2

Mom's Reality Interweaves Into Her Sister's Demise

Miserable comforters are ye all.

Job 16:2

First thing in the morning, after milking, feeding and helping Aunt Linda get the kids off on the bus, Daddy called the hospital and got the news. He was overwhelmed with joy—and guilt. He and Aunt Linda left for the hospital as fast as they could go.

Getting there took forever; the traffic was twice as heavy as last night. It was 7:30 AM, the middle of rush hour, which made a big difference.

Both Daddy and Aunt Linda had a conscience, although weak. They sat, fidgeted and didn't look at each other. The radio played. One or the other talked the whole way, so there wouldn't be time to think. Even Aunt Linda could see the guilt from last night's escapade. She would never let him know this, though. They wouldn't admit their own guilt, let alone, each other's.

My father kept on and on about how great all his kids were, how wonderful. He waved his "wonderful" marriage in his sister-in-law's face, without considering her feelings. The way Daddy felt was all that ever mattered to Daddy. He'd been raised to think he was King, Lord and Master, the Head of the House. No one else really counted. No one ever said no to Daddy. He was brought up to believe that Bill Marbello must always win. So he thought he could talk himself out of any situation. Except once, before Mom and him were married, when two police officers explained that no, he could not commit armed robbery and yes, his ass was going to prison for 4 years.

*   *   *

MARIAN'S VADE MECUM

Before we could get married, Bill had to talk to my Mom & Dad, and tell them about his being in prison for armed robbery. They were very understanding. Told him that anyone could make a mistake, but as long as we learned from our mistakes it's okay.

*   *   *

My father was oblivious to his enslavement by not one, but two demons. But, I knew, oh yes, it would make all the difference in his destiny who, ultimately, won soul control. I laughed quietly at my vision of his future. It was my past.

When Daddy paused, inexplicably, to chuckle a little, Aunt Linda ignored her hurt and stated, "The new baby is wonderful news. Babies are so sweet. They can be so cute, can't they and won't it be nice to have more help around the farm. You can always use more hands around the place and, of course, *I'm* glad to help out too, you know. You and Marian are so lucky . . ." She didn't mean one word of it.

Daddy shushed her with a curt gesture as they entered Mom's hospital room.

Mom looked a little drained, but even after having a baby, she was doing well. She had just finished breastfeeding little Jake.

He was a beautiful infant, with his dark, Italian complexion and dark, brown eyes. He had lots of black hair and was long for a newborn. I must say, they were pleased and very proud parents—for totally different reasons. To Daddy, it was one more proof of what a man he was. The rule was, the more sons you had, the more virile you were, and everybody could see it every Sunday in church. He sent the rest of the family every single Sunday, but hardly ever went by himself. There was always "a good reason" why he couldn't or wouldn't. To Mom, it was the satisfaction of bringing another beautiful and healthy baby in the world to please her man.

Phony Aunt Linda held out her arms as she ran around the side of the bed to hug her sister. Fake as a shopping mall Santa.

"Oh Marian, honey, how are you doing? Are you all right? How's the baby?" Then, she watched Daddy like a hawk while he interacted with his wife. Her jealousy of her only sister was so strong that it made her a bitter, cold person on the inside. On the outside, she put on a huge Kool-Aid front, artificially flavored, colored and loaded with sugar.

Aunt Linda couldn't have kids, but she didn't know that. She was always sipping on sodas and it inevitably gave her the worst bladder infections. These infections became so frequent and severe that they affected her ovaries, so now there were some cysts on them.

Bless my Mother's heart—she looked so worn out. I actually felt sorry for her, along with a twinge of what was probably tenderness or protectiveness. I wasn't sure. The sensations were unfamiliar and disorienting to me. *Was this my introduction to human emotions?*

Mom turned to Daddy. "The doctor's going to discharge me soon. I can't wait to get home." Aunt Linda's eyes narrowed.

Daddy knew he'd better do something fast, so he told Mom, "Aw, really now, honey, by the time they get you discharged and get all the prescriptions filled and everything, it's going to be too late, on account of the kids coming off the bus at a quarter to four. That's pretty soon, you know, and they don't know Joe that good . . . well, I don't guess there's time to wait, sorry." He shrugged it off, knowing that it would be the way he wished.

Mom groaned in disappointment, so Aunt Linda said quickly, "I'd be more than happy to help out with the kids and spend the night again." Of course, she had to elaborate and went on and on. "Oh, now don't fret yourself, Marian, I'll make sure the kids get their showers and do their homework . . . tell you what, I could even spring for pizza." She looked meaningfully at Daddy. "A *large* one, with *extra* toppings."

Daddy tried not to leer as Rashma moved in his groin.

Mom smiled as Aunt Linda knew she would. The kids loved pizza from the Pizza Hut in Old Town and didn't get it often. It was forty-five minutes away from the dairy farm, almost in Bangor.

"Okay, then, you all go on, now. I need my rest," said Mom, still smiling. She only said what was required to get the job done. Daddy and Aunt Linda were the really mouthy ones.

The nurse had already taken Jake off for display in the nursery goo-goo gaga window. Aunt Linda said her goodbyes, so she could find a phone and call in the pizza order. Daddy said his good-byes in two seconds and was out in the hall, after Aunt Linda. He couldn't even wait until they reached the car, before his hand slid up her skirt, grabbing her ass. These two *deserved* each other.

Ecclesiastes 7:26

Linda Hayes felt triumph as she hurried to the car with Daddy. *Bill Marbello is mine again,* she thought, *at least for the time being.* She intended it to be permanent, for she was so envious of Mom's seemingly happy, stable situation with Daddy. Not as envious of the kids that you were supposed to have if you got married, but they came with the territory. It was the security and companionship that she wanted.

I knew all about Aunt Linda's motives, because I had been watching her for years as well. Her crush on Daddy had started in high school.

Daddy didn't bother to open the car door for Aunt Linda— they just jumped in and took off. They picked up the pizza and got home before the school bus.

It wouldn't have been life or death, if they had gotten home slightly late, for Jackie was getting older now and she was a bright, responsible girl. Mom shoved off all the work on little Jackie after school; that she could get away with, anyway. She had to. She had her hands full with the kids, the cooking, the dishes, her garden and her husband. Daddy did the same thing with the oldest boy, waking him at 4 a.m. and working him until he fell asleep in the hayloft and on the backs of sleeping cows, in stolen moments of rest.

The bus pulled up, and the kids came tearing out of it, yippee, yi yawing and carrying on with Lobo, who was a barker and a jumper, just like the kids. It was chaos, as Daddy came into the house; the kids and Lobo were going crazy for pizza, jumping and yelling. Aunt Linda and Daddy easily drowned them all out.

Aunt Linda snapped, *"Hey!"* and Daddy yelled, "All of you shut the *hell up!"* The kids shut up, but the dog barked more, so Daddy kicked him out.

Jackie imitated her elders and got going on her brothers. In her bossy, teasing way, she told them they had to wait. Now you know The Rules. Eight o'clock, after chores, that's when you can have it and not one minute before.

The kids did know The Rules, for they had been beaten into them. They'd be scarred for life by those unbreakable Rules in all kinds of ways. For one thing, the kids only had half an hour to change from school clothes to work clothes, eat a snack and play around a little, before it was time for the dreaded after-school regime.

To escape the three-ring circus, Aunt Linda ambled into the dining room and set the pizza up on top of the upright freezer Mom had in there. She was relieved that she didn't have kids yet, which would force her to put up with the racket in the kitchen twenty-four hours a day. It was bad enough that she had to put up with it for this short while.

She walked back into the kitchen and winked at Jackie, who smiled in return. Linda was jealous of the attention Daddy showed his oldest and of the closeness that they shared as father and daughter. But she also knew that the only way to remain in Daddy's favor was to stay on Jackie's good side. Just as Jackie knew that she had to please Aunt Linda, no matter what, for the same reason.

Everyone in the house buried their true feelings most of the time.

Tonight was going to be very strange . . . I could tell that something wasn't right, I just had this feeling from Rashma. In his head, huge invisible gears were working.

By this time, I was beginning to read and understand Rashma a little better. I'd just fed on the poor little bastard's soul. He thought that he had the power to hold me off, but he was wrong. Soon, he wouldn't even have the power to leave this body without my approval. With a little more time, I could squish him down and use him to generate power for my ultimate being, my thrust into the next world.

I can't wait to become my very own vampire in human form with hot blood running through my veins, experiencing the sweet smells of Mother Earth and partaking of all the riches that our Precious Lord put here for us. It is only a matter of time now before I take communion with you, your reality, and your world.

The more wicked Daddy felt, the louder he preached and proclaimed his godliness. My presence was obviously having an impact on him—he was talking to Matthew in the barn about taking him to Bible school.

He then slithered up to the house to tell Jackie how pretty she was and how grown-up she looked when she was in the kitchen, baking. Jackie was standing on a chair pulled over to the stove, so she could reach the pot she was stirring. She was making Mom's homemade rice pudding. She was also keeping an eye on her two youngest brothers who were at the table being themselves, calling each other names, throwing wadded napkins and trying to kick each other.

The little, seven-year-old girl was on her best behavior, because of the Pizza Hut Pizza dinner planned for tonight and she felt guilty, letting it slip to Aunt Linda that Daddy had let her try a couple puffs of his cigarette. Earlier while they were baking cookies, Jackie had confided that "Daddy doesn't care if I smoke cigarettes, Aunt Linda. He says he thinks I look cute when I try to blow smoke rings. He showed me how to French inhale, too." .

Daddy switched tactics and pretended to get angry. "Now, dammit to hell, Jackie, don't you go telling anyone about you play-smoking, you hear me?" He knew she already had. Aunt Linda had wasted no time in betraying her niece. Ole Daddy just held it over Jackie's head as one more thing to manipulate her with—he enjoyed doing that to people.

Aunt Linda heard Daddy's voice and came down from upstairs. She was dolled up in lacy, hot pink lingerie and high-heeled slippers from a place called SEXY STUF, full makeup and a suffocating cloud of Jungle Gardenia. They do spell it with only one F.

It was all Daddy could do to say that he had to go to the barn. He was a horny bastard, all right.

By the time Daddy reached the barn, Matthew was finishing up on the milking part of his chores. Matthew, like the rest of the kids, born and yet to be born, was so small when he started milking cows that Daddy had to put a wooden bench along each side of the cement barn floor, so that he could stand on it just to reach the cows' titties (teats).

We had about 125 cows total; milked 75 full time, the rest were mostly dry and of course we always had a few fresh ones to contend with.

Matthew still had to feed the hogs and baby calves, run the milked cows out to pasture, wash down the parlor, change gates around and wash up the calf buckets. After Matthew was finished with the buckets, Daddy would wash the milking machines himself, running all kinds of solutions through them to sterilize them. We all worked very hard to sell our grade A milk.

The afternoon passed quickly and now it was around eight o'clock. The kids had to eat, shower, do their homework and maybe catch some playtime before ten o'clock. That was their butts-upstairs-to-bed time for six hours of sleep and if they didn't go, they were in trouble. Daddy was damned strict. The kids enjoyed their pizza and promised that when they got through; they would do their homework and go to bed.

The two oldest kids were warming up to Daddy all right. They scurried about as fast as they could, putting all of their homework on the kitchen table. Before Daddy could say much, they had their heads right down, almost into their books, so Daddy let them study, almost believing that they were capable of it. Matthew, who was in kindergarten, wasn't getting graded yet, but he wasn't doing too good. His goody-two-shoes sister, Jackie, who was in first grade, was getting good grades of A's, B's and C's, plus Aunt Linda had helped her with her homework earlier. This made Matthew hate her that much more.

Aunt Linda got up and asked if Daddy would please come into the other room with her, because she wanted to talk to him. His nostrils flared like a hound on the trail, and he followed closely behind, inhaling Jungle Gardenia, as they went around the corner into the dining room.

My mother used this room for everything but dining. It was the baby's room and sewing room, with a big freezer along one wall. In one corner was Mom's desk, a junk pile from hell. Aunt Linda was getting right to the point when Jerrod waddled into the room with his bottom lip stuck out. Jason, that big, fat bully, had hit him. Thank goodness it was dark in the corner and Jerrod didn't really see much. All he knew was that Aunt Linda was on Daddy's lap.

When they were caught, Aunt Linda flew right off Daddy and turned her back. Daddy stood up and tried to fit himself back into his pants. It wasn't easy, but he did finally manage to get zipped up, turned around and proceeded to chew out Jerrod. Before he really got going, Aunt Linda interrupted quickly to let Daddy know that she had to call home to see if her pets were okay. A friend was staying with her white, Maltese Chan Chan and her love birds, Bushy Butt and Petrey.

My father started acting nervous, like a cornered cat, not knowing which way to go or what to do next. I knew Rashma was the cause, for he was starting to feel weird and agitated to me. Finally, Daddy suggested to Aunt Linda that he was going to do his late chores now and stressed that it would be nice if she cleared the table and got the kids in bed.

Daddy was a hard worker and taught his kids to be as well. He always went back outside at night, usually when the kids went to bed, to grind feed. His ironclad nighttime routine also never failed to include one final check on things outside.

Tonight, when Daddy opened the door, a soft wind was rolling across the back porch, like a small, refreshing burst of the Santa Ana in Maine. All the beautiful stars were out, singing songs of twinkling, soft light. He turned winked at Aunt Linda and proceeded across the lawn.

Out of the darkness, a pale, blur streaked straight for my Dad. I knew something was up, but I wasn't expecting this, nor was Daddy.

Lobo gave himself away by growling.

Daddy heard him just in time and kicked out as hard as he could with his steel-toed boot. Whimpering, tail tucked between his legs, Lobo ran as fast as he could to the calf barn, where he could hide in safety.

"Jesus Christ, Almighty!" Daddy was flabbergasted. His own dog had just attacked him and he cussed in bewilderment all the way to the grain room.

Of course, it was me and Rashma that Lobo was going for.

Right as my father switched on the lights in the feed room, he could hear two or three packs of coyotes from the distant, rolling hills of timber. He roamed around, trying to find some more urea to put with the grain. He was looking behind sacks of all-purpose minerals, when a huge rat jumped out and landed on his upper arm, plopped to the floor and ran out the open door.

"Jesus Christ, I'll be a son of a bitch!" Daddy said in disgust as he reached for the electric button to start all the grain augers, rollers and grinders. The precise moment that he hit the button, his knees, legs and everything came out from under him as if all the energy was being sucked out of his body at once. Grain was flying out from one of the full hoppers, landing all over him and the floor.

There was an enormous hopper in the corner, the top opening at floor level and the rest of it going about fifteen feet down into the ground. Used for bulk feed, it had a gigantic auger at the bottom that would take the grain to a waiting, feed truck.

When the large motor started up on the big, floor hopper, he started yelling for help. But no one in the house could hear him as the auger went faster and faster and got louder and louder, the floor shaking worse than a California earthquake. His body started to vibrate toward the hopper. He tried with all the strength in his being to reach out and grasp the leg of a blue, Fibercon wheelbarrow. The wheelbarrow was bouncing up and down and moving from side to side, as if it had a mind of its own. It started to move toward him like it was going to push him down into the hopper. He stretched out both arms to grab the wheelbarrow, threw it over himself and down into the hopper. The noise was horrendous, screeching, groaning and clanking, as the augur chewed everything up and spit it out the other side. At least now, Daddy wasn't in the middle of the floor. He maneuvered to the side, clutched the leg of an upright, steel hopper and hung on for dear life.

So, this was what Rashma wanted. He wanted to talk. I could read his mind. Damn him for doing that. He knew that this was almost his end, for my powers were becoming stronger and stronger every day. If Rashma didn't prove his point soon, he might never be able to. He wanted to make a deal with me, one that would expel him from my father's body, forever.

I had planned to use Rashma right on down, till there was nothing left of his soul, but a memory. If I chose not to agree with him, Daddy would be ground up like hamburger.

Two demons fighting within can cause fatal havoc in a human's body.

The screeching, whining noises got even louder, as the deadly blades spun faster, creating a wind. The horrible shaking got stronger as though everything was going to fly apart and blow away. Daddy's hands started to slip, as his whole body rose off the floor from Rashma's coercion. Rashma already had Daddy's legs out in mid-air, directly over the edge of the hungry, floor hopper. He could not hang on any longer. His body strength had been completely sucked out of him.

He started to give up and let go, when, as quickly as it started, it stopped. Everything shut down at once, leaving me wondering what Rashma might be up to next. The only noise was Daddy, crying on the floor, still holding the steel leg with all his might. After a time, he raised up on his elbows and then, got up from his knees to stagger around, stupefied. His mind was blank.

It was starting to get late. Aunt Linda had already put the kids to bed quite some time ago and was waiting for Daddy. She was twenty-four, unmarried and getting anxious. Her religion programmed men and women to believe that women are good for one thing, to get married and have lots of babies and forgive whatever their husbands chose to dish out.

Linda didn't even like children much, merely tolerating them when she had to. She thought they were stupid, and they got on her nerves. She was cold, quick and curt with the kids—unless Daddy was nearby. Then, and only then, was she all smiles, hugs, and kisses toward them.

Aunt Linda knew she needed to snag a husband to have any respect whatsoever from her peers and her sister's husband would do nicely. She would use the only ammunition she had -

sex and a pregnancy. She missed her pantsuit and flat, comfortable shoes, but it was all for a good cause. She felt ridiculous, but she knew Daddy would like it.

When Aunt Linda heard the screen door open, she did her best to arrange her stocky body into a seductive pose. Daddy ignored her and promptly excused himself to go shower, before she had a chance to see the scuffs and scratches on his face and hands. She was becoming impatient. It took a lot of work to look like this and she didn't appreciate waiting around.

Chubby Jason came down from upstairs, crying. "Aunt Linda, a boogey man is going to come into the house. I can feel it. I'm scared, Aunty Linda."

As she tried not to break her neck in the darn, high heels on the way back upstairs, Aunt Linda told him it was only a bad dream, no reason to worry, go back to bed and get some sleep. She left his room quickly, before the obnoxious pipsqueak started squalling about the boogey man again. . .

Aunt Linda had seen the attic door next to Mom and Daddy's room many times before. But . . . why <u>this</u> night, did it seem to be staring at her, watching her? Chills ran all the way up and down her whole body. She wrapped her arms around herself, as if she was cold and started walking toward the attic door. It was like some force kept her walking slowly toward the door and her hand was almost on the knob, when she heard Daddy open the bathroom door. The spell broken, Linda moved unsteadily into the bedroom and waited for Daddy to come in.

Daddy, meanwhile, was trying to put what had just happened to him out of his mind. When he emerged from the bathroom, completely naked, he looked at Aunt Linda for the first time and couldn't believe how beautiful she looked. His eyes raked her body. She rolled over and sat up, getting closer to the edge of the bed, so he could approach. Their eyes met, intensifying the pressure in Daddy's groin.

His swollen member was throbbing up and down as he stood in front of her. Without a word, he got down and put his arms around her, laying her back down on the bed with one arm. He then lowered her onto her back, so she ended up under him, with her legs wrapped around his tight waist.

At this time, I could feel Rashma's presence like never before. Yes, I *did* underestimate him. I felt pressure. It was Rashma pushing with all his might, *trying to get into Aunt Linda*. This was his last chance, and he knew that if he didn't do this, he would have to submit to me again, for I was the more powerful demon. The one who could feed on him, eating his soul away, until nothing was left but a void, that went to nowhere and belonged unto no place.

When I first got into Daddy, I should have crushed Rashma and thrown him out without even part of a soul to feed on, for stealing this man's body—especially, after I had waited so long for my chance. But I was greedy and wanted to use all of his powers to help ensure my new adventure. Now, he planned on stealing my idea of transforming into a human to become a living vampire.

Except it seemed that Rashma didn't know that Aunt Linda couldn't have any children. Before I could, against my better judgment, warn him, Rashma was gone. In a way, it felt as if he had taken some of my strength with him . . . Surely, Rashma hadn't tried to feed on *my* soul?

I still had time to build myself up, though, for the day that I had targeted for my conception was December 1, 1962.

"Just give me a few more minutes," Aunt Linda said to Daddy the next morning as he tried for the third time to wake her. She wasn't feeling well at all. Two trips already early this morning to the bathroom to puke, made her feel weak and nauseated. He shook her again.

"Hey, Linda! It's getting late, I can't wait any longer. I'll go get Marian by myself, but dammit, I expect you, Little Miss Play

Sick, to straighten up your act. You have to help out with things in the house for a few days now. So get up, dammit. My wife needs all the help she can get around here." He turned and walked out the door to bring home Mom and the new baby, Jake.

Still feeling sick to her stomach, Aunt Linda managed to get up, out of bed and go down the hall into the bathroom. She looked up into the mirror, and then noticed her horrible breath, which smelled like something rotten down in her throat. When she reached for the toothbrush to clean her teeth, a sharp stabbing got her, right in the middle of her abdomen. She automatically doubled over with excruciating pain, dropping her toothbrush. She hung on to the door jam, head spinning and looked toward the bedroom to see if her strength could take her all the way back onto the wonderful bed.

On the way to the hospital, Daddy kept thinking about last night. In all his thirty-five years, he'd never had an acid burning sensation when having an orgasm. It also crossed his mind that Mom would be pissed at him for not calling and checking up on her. He always had the perfect answer for her and the sad thing is: she always so innocently believed him. I made Daddy look up into the rear-view mirror, to see for myself, the cold, angry, blue-green glow of his evil, possessed eyes. He had entered an empty world, powerless unto my control, mine to feed on and to manipulate.

At the hospital, Mom was ready and had been waiting for a while. The head nurse had already made sure that Mom had the prescribed things from her doctor, got her paperwork ready to go and even found a wheelchair for her.

Mom got a little perturbed when her door opened and one of the other nurses came in. She was expecting Daddy.

Yes, it took Daddy a while, because he was easily distracted by a cute blonde at the elevators. He held the elevator door open as it jerked back and forth. This was the back entrance to the

Maternity Ward, so there wasn't anyone else around. They flirted with each other for a good twenty-five minutes or so. Finally, a bell went off on one of the other elevators. This was her cue to get rid of him, so she excused herself and at the same time, removed his hand from the door, so it could close.

He took a deep breath and did a playful half-kick, skip and yelp to shake all the guilt and come back down to earth before he got to Mom's room.

Mom could hear him coming, so she started to get up and go for Baby Jake, fast asleep in his bassinet, over by the corner. She was reaching for him as Daddy walked in with arms outstretched and a big smile on his face, pretending to fulfill the role of proud father to a tee. He helped her into the wheelchair, swung Mom's bag over his shoulder, put Baby Jake into her arms and wheeled her to the car, with a nurse running behind him. He was such an impatient man, zooming on past the Nurse's Station, without even giving Mom a chance to say good-bye to anyone.

Traffic was heavy, but the drive home didn't take long, although they were in no rush, since two of the kids weren't due home for quite some time yet. Joe was watching the younger ones, as usual. It was a harmonious ride home for Daddy. Mom didn't lay into him at all about not calling last night, talking instead of things she'd do when she got everything back to normal.

A virtuous woman is a crown to her husband:
Proverbs 12:4

*　　*　　*

I always had a garden, canned everything I could get my hands on. I helped in the fields and with the cows. I kept all the cow and calf records. Paid all the bills. Bill just worked. He was only home on weekends. We never went out at all. To many children and cows.

* * *

Deep concern crept across Daddy's face, as he realized Aunt Linda's problem with helping Mom out around the house. That morning, he'd known she was sick and was only kidding, telling her in his way to get well quickly, but he knew better. He was thinking, *Yeah, probably a damn, bad case of the flu,* when Mom, looking green, said she was grateful that the farm was only around a couple more corners in the windy road.

Poor Mom, she was deathly ill from carsickness. It had to do with the abnormal equilibrium in her ears. She was trying not to throw up on her new baby.

Lost in thoughts of Aunt Linda, Daddy realized that the car was going too fast for the upcoming curve and slammed his foot on the brake pedal, almost forcing Mom and Jake into the dashboard. She screamed in fright, *"Bill,* for God's sake in Heaven—watch where you're going!"

Aunt Linda was up and getting about the best she could, aware that the impending introduction of the new baby would throw the damnable house into pandemonium. Daddy always announced the arrival, as he personally carried it proudly across the threshold. *The way he carries on,* she sighed, *you'd think he was solely responsible for its birth.*

Linda was in dire straits, but still managed to pull the bedcovers up, so Mom wouldn't notice she'd been sleeping in there with Daddy. She never thought about stripping the sheets.

On the way to the bathroom again, in the hallway, a wrenching pain hit her lower stomach area, so piercing that it contorted her face, doubled her over and collapsed her to the floor. Hyperventilating, she could hear them pulling up to the house. With all the fortitude she could muster, Linda headed into the bathroom and proceeded to wash her face and brush her hair.

It was an unpleasant ride for Mom, but they made it home, so she was happy. Coming around the car to open the door for Mom, Daddy noticed Aunt Linda peering out of the bathroom window. He had to pay attention to Mom, now, by holding the baby, while she held his arm. They walked up the pea gravel cement sidewalk to the front porch.

Bill Marbello was egotistical and narcissistic when it came to himself. That was the main reason for doing his proclamation, upon crossing the threshold. It was for him, not his children. Poor Mom didn't know the difference. She was just glad to be in her own element. Home, sweet home, was truly where her heart was.

She put tiny Jake down to rest in the cluttered dining room, inside his well-used crib, snug as a bug in a rug. Daddy paced the kitchen floor, angered that Aunt Linda hadn't washed the dishes. He kept looking through the dining room, to see if she was coming downstairs. Mom tried to get all the dishes pushed aside on the counter, ready to wash. It wasn't easy. They were piled up like Mt. Everest. As patient as Mom was, though, she just slowly started on them and was making, at least, some progress.

With half an ear, she listened to Daddy as he rambled on about going upstairs to see what was keeping Aunt Linda, for she should have been down by now and he couldn't believe she wasn't there for his little ceremony on the porch.

Just about ready to come out of the bathroom, Aunt Linda had finished changing out of blood-soaked panties into some clean ones, when the door opened. It was Daddy. As he looked down, he could see all the blood in her other stained underwear, as she washed them in the vanity. She scolded him for not knocking, as did he, her, for taking so long. He could see what the problem was now, a female thing and started to leave, without any concern for the situation. *ILL* and irritated at his callousness, Aunt Linda muttered that this wasn't her time of the month for this to happen, but he was already out the bathroom door, going downstairs to join Mom in the kitchen.

Aunt Linda sighed, slightly miffed at his predictable, single-minded focus on Mom now that she and the new baby were home. Although she had promised Mom a couple of days of help, she just wanted to get out of there and take care of herself, so she cleaned up the bathroom the best she could and went back into the bedroom for her bags.

Daddy was almost finished telling Mom about her sister, when Linda walked into the room with her bags. Mom understood completely and helped Daddy reassure Aunt Linda that she shouldn't feel guilty about leaving so soon. Linda went on to say that she also didn't want the new baby to get sick, so she would see him another time. Giving to them each a hug, she was soon driving down the two-mile gravel driveway, her car whining down, as she shifted for the corners. After a moment, it was only a faint hum and then it distanced itself, without an audible trace.

Aunt Linda was almost to the Baxter State Park and doing well over the speed limit, as she headed west on 157 when she zoomed by a road sign that read, *Rest Area One Mile*. Her focus was getting back to her own bed . . . *bed! Oh God, I didn't tell Bill about the* bed. *Jesus—maybe it isn't too late to try and let him know.* It was probably the only rest area until she got back home, so she pulled in to use the telephone. Her spasms had alleviated for a bit, but as she went in first to use the bathroom, she was not prepared for what she discovered—her clean underwear, worn for only two hours, was soaked with blood. It shocked her so much that panicky tears ran down her face. She didn't know what to do, except run back out to the car for her night bag, clean up and get home as quickly as possible. Making the call slipped from her mind.

Later that afternoon, when Mom went upstairs and saw her bed, she knew that Linda had slept there. *What a gentleman Bill was*, she thought, *to have slept on the sofa!* She smiled lovingly as she did the laundry.

The days folded into weeks and by three and a half months into her pregnancy, Linda was acting almost intoxicated, judging by the way she walked around, elated over carrying Daddy's baby. It was too much for her to handle, because she knew good and well that she was falling into premium love with her sister's husband. Everything had gone stupendously for her lately. Marveling, she relished the fact that she now would have a lasting hold on Daddy's soul.

This was her moment of bliss, but how much longer could she keep the identity of her baby's father a secret? Her sister couldn't find out. It would be a sin she'd never forgive, and she would relegate her to the depths of Hell. Besides which, Daddy warned Linda that if she was to spill it or let it leak in any way, she would be "one sorry, dejected woman that wouldn't be getting her essential desires taken care of anymore." He also told her that she would be cast out of her sister's family. He told her she should pray over it.

Daddy had already covered his own ass by telling the "Big Lie" about Linda and how a guy broke into her house, beat her up and raped her, leaving her pregnant.

Unequivocally and indubitably, nothing outshined waking up on a Sunday morning to the delightful aroma of Mom's homemade blueberry pancakes. The berries she used were succulent, making a light blue, effervescent batter. The kids could hardly wait. When a steaming, hot stack of them hit the table, they went crazy, like they were in a shark feeding frenzy. They reached and grabbed and drowned the pancakes with Mom's special homemade maple syrup and dairy creamery butter.

After breakfast, everyone had to gussy up for church. Today, in a rare exception to his "no church for me, but everyone else must go" rule, Daddy was going with the family. While it was easier for the boys and Daddy to get ready, since Mom and Jackie had to clean up the kitchen before they could titivate, the women still looked seemly, as befitted the occasion. compared to the men, who only dressed because they had to.

Everyone loved to turn around in their pews and watch the blooming Marbello lineage walk up the aisle. It helped fill up the pews and the young children were quite a contrast to the oppressive, elderly congregation. The real reason they went, of course, is so Daddy could parade his healthy crop of progeny and be admired or envied.

Normally, the family would go straight home after church. However, today, the kids got to visit their grandparents, Nanna and Pappa Marbello. They lived about two miles behind the farm. The kids had walked it many times. Arriving was invariably a blast for the children, with dogs jumping up, ducks waddling around and chickens darting everywhere. The children's taste buds were all set for the goodies Nanna always had.

The Marbello grandparents loved all their grandchildren dearly, but the youngsters were always at school or forever working on the farm. They didn't get to see as much of them as they would have liked, so they would consistently ham it up with them. They were fun to be with.

Almost in a snap, it was time to say good-bye. Daddy, Mom and the kids had to get home to the chores and dinner and some of the kids had school early in the morning. The children had to work every Saturday, go to Sunday school, plus church, attend regular school all during the week, be in all the church functions—and still try, with all their hearts, to be only kids.

*　　*　　*

MARIAN'S VADE MECUM

The children went to Sunday School every Sunday. What ever was going on at school or church with the children I always had to go, Bill wouldn't. He also wouldn't go to church with us. Then I would fix stuff for a picnic at the lake. Our kids didn't get to do very much, then at the last minute Bill would back out, and tell me that he wouldn't go. It really hurt the kids, and me. After a while, if he wouldn't go with us, I just took the children and went anyhow. I always told him when we were going, and let him know that he was welcome. But he never came. Bill always made promises to us all, and never kept them from day one.

*　　*　　*

Mom was on the sofa relaxing in front of the television, as she waited for Daddy to finish tucking in the children, before she went up to bed. He had already said their prayers to them and tonight, instead of turning toward his bedroom, he went through the small door, up the curved staircase and into the attic. That is to say, I, Morbose, went to the attic. Daddy had no choice but to come along.

When she found herself dozing off, Mom got off the sofa, locked the doors, turned out lights and started up the stairs for bed, where she assumed Daddy was. Just as Mom got to the top steps, the phone rang. She went back downstairs to answer it. Up in the attic, Daddy couldn't hear the phone ringing almost off the hook. Mom got to it, before it woke the kids.

It was Nanna, wanting to let Mom know that she was coming over in the morning to help out some. Mom said that would be fine and started upstairs, again. By the time she reached her room, Daddy was already in bed, asking what took her so long. She told him what his mother had said, which made Daddy feel better about snuggling up for the night.

*   *   *

MARIAN'S VADE MECUM

All the years we were married I never refused him Sex. Even after and right before my children were born. I don't care how tired I was. And he always hurt me when we made love. I don't know why it hurt, but it did. Now it don't hurt me when Weasel makes love to me. And we last a lot longer, up to 2 hrs. Average is about ½ to ¾ of an hour. It seems like I always wanted Sex, but then it would hurt.

*   *   *

Chapter 3

The Devil's Bible

NOW is the time for me to bequeath unto you some of the truths about me, for you have a right to know. I, Morbose, the trusted Red Devil Demon, was locked in pure Hell for torturous centuries that turned into epochs to eons of torment. This was rapturous bliss for the Devil, whom I must call God of the Underworld, the mightiest angel of them all, for eternity the beautiful King Of Demons, my Father, my Lucifer.

It is wise to worship the powers that be or seem to, wherever you are.

The Beast took great concealment in all his disguises, and no one ever saw him change from one being to the next. Millions of Red Devil Demons discussed it endlessly in the archaic style of speech used in the Underworld. For, we all knew him to look barbaric, with shiny, large, curved bull horns protruding from his inhuman head. His skin was red and black, as if it was glossy, patent leather illuminating a slick gleam of light. He had gargantuan shoulders with extensive, cerise wings etched in ebony. Immense arms ended in stalwart hands, with long, incurvate fingernails. His torso was that of a muscular, rippled, well-endowed human and a pitch-black loincloth of sorts, covered the lower part of it with a big, red chain around his waist. He strutted on sinewy, red hairy legs and cloven hooves, personifying the libidinous, indomitable evil, seen only in Hell.

One of the verses that he used to tantalize me with, time and time again, tells of his "confinement" within Hell's boundaries:

> *For it says it in the Devil's Bible that when God cast him forevermore down into the pit of hell, The only light that shineth may be the light of the darkest cave behind the unyielding Chateau in the Hades, for he may NOT go out unto Earth the Garden of Eden itself.*
> **Acts of God:**

He can't come to you, but you can go to him. When you are sent to Hell, you are instantly excoriated like a piece of fruit. Everything about you is taken; even your name and you are given another. Nothing is left, but a small soul of energy that Lucifer feeds on and then turns into a Red Devil Demon or the highest of persuasive demons, a Possessor like me. He has to turn you into a Red Devil Demon or he would not be able to see you to consume your soul. The souls that Lucifer uses for his feeding, give power and wealth to his everlasting entity.

Even Lucifer himself cannot completely consume every last speck of life in a soul. After he's depleted your power, he sets your soul free, to go out into the cosmos to help create energy. You work your way back into the evolution of life again, trying desperately to find an existence. Until then, you are at his mercy, for who knows how long.

But the very hairs of your head are all numbered.
St. Matthew 10:30

Red Devil Demons are pure red, with small, curved, yellow-flicked horns. They possess a demonic look to their faces, with jagged, sharp, spiked teeth. On the tops of their heads are tufts of red hair, as well as on the end of their prehensile tails. They have bodies, legs, arms and feet similar to humans, although demons slouch considerably more. Nor do they have wings like Lucifer, who could fly, simply by holding his wings out.

Since all of them are the same sex, it is a true pit of carnality, against a backdrop of an eternity spent in senseless agony and self-torture. If one of them wanted to burn itself away or slice its neck, it could try, but it would feel the pain—for it cannot die, only continue to suffer even more.

Thousands upon millions cannot take it anymore and try to commit suicide, thinking they can get into the Beyond. They only end up writhing deeper into the depths of how bad Hell can really be: waiting again, for Lucifer's empty promises, imploring him to eat their suffering souls, hoping the pain will end.

Not so long ago, I can remember walking down through the corridors of Hell with my Lucifer. He wanted me to walk with him as he paraded in front of his countless crops of captive souls. We watched as they wriggled and tossed back and forth, shrieking and wailing in pure agony. While we walked on, through tunnels and over many bridges, others were chortling, snorting and groaning in animalistic fornication, right beside piles of their own sickening waste. The whole place was lit up from the burning fires of Hell, casting a red glow on the surfaces of everything and hurtling sharp shadows into the corners and small caverns. The stink of decomposing demon flesh and reeking waste was unbearable. One did not merely retch—one puked one's guts out onto the slimy floor.

I knew that while almighty Lucifer could oversee everything that happened in his domain with his mind, he could not read my mind and that's all I had left. That is what brought me to Mother Earth—my want and desire to be a breathing, living vampire. As I guarded his evil throne for so many years, I finally came upon the secret, so well hidden for eons; *how to escape from Hell.*

I watched and kept my mouth shut and it got me through PURE Hell. The demons, his followers said his Bible held all the secrets to the Devil's powers that it would reveal the way out. Countless, unwary souls who looked for it ended up forever feeding Lucifer's hungry demand for power.

The chosen ones of the Red Devil Demons guarded his iniquitous throne. He chose the smartest, most powerful ones, for if they flunked the test of trust, he would devour their souls.

I could not take that chance. I didn't want to start over in life, being a part of some space energy. That wasn't enough for me, not after Lucifer himself, it tantalized me with the secret of . . . *vampirism.*

Once the Red Devil Demons pass the test, they are sent out onto the earth, as disembodied demons. As they enter the Cavern CITH (Château In The Hades), meaning Castle in Hell, they became demons that possess and do the Devil's bidding for him. Their sole purpose is to acquire. I passed the test, time after time, even knowing what family and everything that I wanted to possess, and he still, through empty promises, never let me go unto the earth. The biggest test of all was knowing his Bible was near but also knowing that one mustn't look for it or one would get the wrath of the deathless Beast.

This, I will tell you the best way I can, how, after hundreds of years working for him, not once, did I look for the Bible. He watched my every move closely. He started to favor me, showing silent attention at first. Then, one day, he came up close behind me as I was on duty guarding the square black throne. It resembles a polished, granite tombstone, set atop a marble mausoleum. Lucifer breathed heavily onto the back of my neck. He told me that none had ever gained his trust as I had. He could take care of my demonic concupiscence and last—but not at all least—he wooed me with verses from his diabolical Bible. He started to tell me, Morbose, the very *page* in the Bible with the secret to entering the Cavern CITH. I was unable to stand it any longer, for I knew how to transceive—he had already told me. All I needed now was to find the entrance to CITH.

The hatred that built inside of me was real, as he teased me, telling of how the Bible radiates a blue light and one has only to think of a verse and it appears to you all lit up, without having to turn a page. Now, he came in even closer, with his bestial mouth to my ear, telling me the verse to call for in the Bible of Hell. The magic words that I needed to break the curse, so I could go on through, into the Cavern of CITH. I knew what was about to happen.

He lust with his father:
Secrets of All:

I moved over to the throne, as he sat down, turned to me and said, "Come here, my most trusted one of all. Come up here onto your Father, for I will tell of the secret passage words to your existence into the Beyond."

I got up on his lap and groin area, where I could see the huge, raging devil-hood pulsating, pushing its way out of the loincloth, exposing its humongous entirety.

Laying me down upon my back on top of his knees, he started to push his massive hardness into my lustful, yearning succulence, moaning, as he enlivened my hunger, like only one other species that I know of, Man, just lustful Man. Lucifer was enthralled by his indulgence. Watching himself penetrate, stimulated him even more. Putting his big hands on my waist, he lifted me up and completely down onto his whole member.

Bending down into my ear, he slowly whispered with bedeviled salacity in his voice, "Your chapter is 'Saint Markus,' my Begotten One. *'Saint Markus'* is what you need to know." He threw back his head with laughter. "All you need now is the Bible of SATAN! Ha ha ha ha."

This sent him into an excessive climax. He groaned, pumping me so full of his fiery, accursed semen that it dripped out, onto his beastly lap. Throwing me down upon the floor and still laughing, he ordered me to get back to my post or lose it to another. Why must I be such a fool, as to trust him, only for him, to mock my very existence? Although, maybe he was telling the truth, thinking I'd never believe him anyway. He *is* the Master of Trickery. So . . . all I need now, is to talk to the Bible— for I know the words that will set me free. I hoped.   . . . But where was it?

I'd thought I was never going to possess the family that I'm in now, the family that I watched for seven years. Now, I knew for sure, I never would. I had acquired his secrets on vampirism. I would never become a Possessor—and knowing how to speak to the Bible of Wickedness was my very own private Hell within Hell.

The day that I found the Bible, Lucifer was out amidst his abandoned, malicious cortege, exhibiting his powers of flight, bellowing loathsome laughter, as he glided over thousands of newly, welcomed souls.

Standing guard, as usual, out in the antechamber, I happened to walk around the corner, just a bit, to get a full view of his throne; a rarity, for no one was allowed in this room, unless the Divine Master himself was in there. The room was empty. Except . . . .

It's not true. No, it can't be. The Most Reverent Words Ever.

Job 42:5

The twelve-inch-thick, black seat of his throne was completely pushed aside from the base. My astounded eyes reflected neon blue light, radiating, coruscating a sapphire gleam up to the ceiling. As I neared the throne, the azure incandescence became paramount, filling the whole room with a white-blue, frosted coldness. I saw it; The Almighty Book of Hell's secrets.

It was my moment and I am quick. Without hesitation, I picked up the wonderful Book. In a loud, stern voice I said, "*Saint Markus.*" Before my voice died away, the wall had dissolved behind his throne. I ran for dear life, through the passage into CITH. I forgot that when the darkest cave shineth its light on a Red Devil Demon, he turns into a Possessor Demon. It was not until the light from the Bible flashed upon me, that I realized I was not red—nor of *any* color, shadowy. *Oh my God in Heaven. What have I done?*

This book in my hands was supposed to be left back inside of the throne's pedestal. The thought of Lucifer's excruciating retribution, kept me from taking the Bible back. That same thought is what made me begin to bury it. There was no other way; if I didn't do something right now, he would find me and take me back to a place I never wanted to visit in my wildest dreams, for the rest of eternity.

I knew he could not see me put cool, musty earth into a heap, directly over the Bible. To him, I was invisible, unless I was red. But I *heard* him, as I covered up the last bit of emitting light.

He raged around a corner of darkness in I don't know what kind of, sadistic, revolting form, inflamed by the fact that he hadn't closed the seat of the throne. Whatever it was came so close, I could feel its searing breath on my demonic face, as it went by.

The days turned into weeks before I finally made contact onto Mother Earth. Finding the way out of CITH was not easy. It goes on for miles and miles of dark, treacherous terrain, under a major city in east Tennessee and snakes under the foothills, rivers and lakes of the Appalachian Mountain Chain.

So, now, I must confess that I stole Lucifer's mightiest power and betrayed his deepest trust. It may lead me into places and things that I cannot dream are possible. But for now, all I want is to live to be born. I didn't mean to take the Devil's Bible, it was a true honest accident, I was overwhelmed as it all took place.

I don't want to end up like Rashma, who is damned to be distorted mentally and physically when he enters the world. I want to be born, like you, with a beautiful, human body. For centuries I've waited, thinking that this will work. It has taken so much to get this far, I will never stop now.

I will have my chance to tell you what it is truly like to be a living-breathing vampire named Markus Antoney Marbello. I will be as honest as I can be in confessing the secrets and telling you the truths of a vampire that will physically stand on your precious Mother Earth.

While on Earth, I want to gain power, knowledge and wealth, for I am not given these things. I am given only the best gift of all—Eternal Life.

I will go back to the Cavern CITH someday, for the blue, glowing Devil's Bible. If it's there, it will be possible for me to learn more about the powers into the Beyond.

For in much wisdom *is* much grief: and he that increaseth knowledge increaseth sorrow.
Ecclesiastes 1:18

Chapter 4

Attic Wall

The harvest is past, the summer is ended, and we are not saved.

Jeremiah 8:20

Thanksgiving was right around the corner and the Marbellos were bustling about. Daddy and Joe were outside, winterizing the barns for the harsh, frigid time, ahead.

As Daddy put insulation over the drainpipe for the pond, all he could think about was Joe. I, myself, was wondering what it would be like to passionately make love with Rashma extinct from my father's body. To experience it for myself, without any interference, captivated my imagination. Only when night falls again will Morbose know the intimate truths about his sensual and seductive behavior.

The incoming cold made it the perfect time of year to be in the house, nice and cozy, especially for Mom. She was on the phone with Linda, begging and demanding at the same time that she was at the family Thanksgiving dinner.

Aunt Linda's guilt was not the only reason that she didn't want to attend Mom's wonderful, give-and-be-thankful dinner. Her lower abdominal pains were starting up again. Yesterday, one of them nailed her to the floor with piercing jabs so powerful that she passed out. She sure didn't want something like that to happen at the dinner, so she just told Mom, "We'll see" and let her go.

Linda was worried. She went into her bedroom to make sure the sleeping pills were in the nightstand. She'd had nights of twisted distress. She tossed and turned, sweating out ragged nightmares. One, in particular, kept recurring; a varmint crawls out of her uterus, its sharp claws sinking in, birthing itself, pulling itself heavily up over her stomach, her chest and to her defenseless neck. All along leaving a fresh heavy thick wet steamy path of womb fluids. It rapaciously starts to satisfy its hunger for blood. Just as slimy incisors sliced into her neck, like a hot knife into butter, she wakes up with both hands around her throat, screaming for help, kicking her legs, as deep, cold sweat saturated her entire body.

What a beautifully blessed, contented Thanksgiving Day this was; life basked itself, the lustrous rays of the sun yielded eternal warmth. It was as if the whole world stopped, just for today. Even the birds in the trees, along with the soft, cool, late autumn breeze, sang songs of happiness, as the music seemed to dance effortlessly, caressing and holding everything for this moment of peace and relaxation.

Things were more hectic than that for Mom, who ran around getting everything together, before the company arrived for dinner. Daddy and the boys watched the Macy's Parade on television, as Jackie unwillingly helped Mom in the kitchen.

* * *

One year at Thanksgiving I had one of the kids in our Scout with me, and I was going to town to buy Groc. for dinner. A big truck threw so much slush at my car, that it made me go off the road. I had Jason in the front seat with me. I held onto him, and I hit my mouth on the steering wheel. It pushed my teeth through my bottom lip, and broke off my 4 front top teeth. I was hurting with my teeth pulled and stitches in my bottom lip, and Bill just laughed. It really hurt me, and made me mad.

Bill borrowed $1,200.00 to get his teeth fixed. He had his glasses. But I needed glasses, and my teeth were breaking off and rotting out of my mouth. But Bill wouldn't do anything or give me any money to have it done. I ended up getting a pair of reading glasses for $10.00 at Wal-Marts. I finally got my teeth worked on after I filed for divorce. He said he would pay for them, but he only paid a couple of hundred dollars and I had to pay the rest of the $5,000.00.

*　　*　　*

Mom was putting the last bit of everything on the table, as the guests started to arrive and she began to wonder if Linda would show up or not. The preacher and his wife were already there. Their neighbors were coming up the walk . . . still, no Aunt Linda.

Knowing that she was late, Aunt Linda drove fast. She was pregnant and preoccupied with how much weight she'd gained and what kind of reactions she would get from family who thought she was raped. It was also a day of lingering pain. Linda devoutly wished it would go away, as she turned into the Marbello's long, gravel driveway. She attempted to concentrate on better things, to put a smile on her face. Ah, herself and Daddy together with their new baby . . . how she would make him leave her sister and get a divorce . . . . Linda felt better, as she pulled up the final stretch of the driveway, toward the big, white farmhouse.

Thanksgiving Dinner was nearly halfway through by the time Aunt Linda slipped into her place at the table. Everyone was going on about how good Mom's food was; of course, she knew this since she and Jackie had made everything on the table from scratch. The country honey-baked ham that Daddy cured, the perfectly cooked wild Canadian goose and the duck, stuffed with wild rice, went splendidly with all the bounty from the garden. You could eat the sugary, sweet pod and all on the French Carouby de Maussane heirloom snow peas as well as the big, juicy, plump, sugar snap peas that Mom always shucked and froze for such an occasion. The potatoes were Russet, mashed to the creamiest, with dairy butter and whole fresh cow's milk and Mom would prepare her marshmallow and sweet potato casserole—the sweet potatoes from her garden, of course. Her turkey dressing was one of a kind; small cubes of potatoes, cooked with lots of sage, hamburger, celery and onion. Very few people do potato dressing, seeming to prefer the more usual bread crumb recipe. Mom smothered fresh, late fall, leaf lettuce with sweetened rich cow's milk and she fixed a wonderful, home grown, Waldorf salad with the perfect amount of black walnuts.

Mom's sourdough, cloverleaf, dinner rolls were the fluffiest ones you could ever put in your mouth. To top it all off, her homemade, country custard, apple pie, sweet, deep, rich pumpkin pie and always, the almost too-sweet, mincemeat pie.

It sure was a feast upon a feast and lasted for two hours. The children indulged themselves, because today, they got to pick what they wanted to eat and talk when they wanted to talk, no matter what, without any interference at all from Mom or Daddy. Most days, they ate sitting silently at the big, long, wooden table, Daddy passed out the food, they ate it and that was that. Sometimes while they ate, Mom would stand behind them with a horse whip. They'd get cracked too, if they spoke out of turn without raising their hand first.

Today, some of the kids didn't finish what was on their plates and giggled, laughed, and babbled out of turn, but no one noticed. With all the company, it was hard to tell who was speaking or laughing and which plate belonged to which person.

After dinner, all the children scampered off to play. Holidays were one of the very few times in their little lives that they had a couple of hours to do whatever their hearts desired. They knew all the adults were helpless, filled like fat ticks and wouldn't be keeping watch much.

*   *   *

MARIAN'S VADE MECUM

Afterwards Bill informed me that he didn't like having all these people over to our house. Said holidays it should just be the ones living at home.

*   *   *

Aunt Linda got up from her chair with a faint groan, excusing herself to go upstairs to use the bathroom. She passed it right by, heading straight for the attic door. She'd wanted to do this for some time now. She opened the door and slowly started walking up the small, curved staircase. The bowed wood creaked underfoot, making her even jumpier than before.

Then, she saw the huge, scratch marks all along the old wallpaper, on each side of the stairs. She about died and was going to turn and flee, when the stairs revealed an open door. Beyond, was an empty room.

The first thing that stood out in this deserted attic was some weird writing on the antique white wallpaper of one wall, lit by the doorway. She then noticed a white bucket with a lid that had some red splatters around the edges below the wall with the writing. Over in a corner, there was an old book of some kind, lying on the floor, smothered in what looked like many, many years of dust sitting all by itself.

Aunt Linda's focus returned to the wall with writing, and she got the heebie-jeebies, for

MORBOSE
TO
MARKUS

was written in large, dripping-wet, fresh blood, running down from every letter, as though just done. When she could bring herself to walk up and touch it, it felt dry. Linda was petrified, frightening vibes shaking her to the core, as she spun and raced to the door. She did not look back at all but headed down the steps as fast as she could, without too much noise.

The guests were about to leave as Aunt Linda walked back into the kitchen looking so odd that Mom asked her if everything was all right. She was six months along, stuffed into jeans, spotting large amounts of blood with horrid cramps and had just seen ghoulish, bloody writing on an attic wall—no, she was *not* all right. Aunt Linda dismissed it, by saying she had too much to eat. They all left to go home, including Aunt Linda, herself, as she gave hugs and kisses, good-bye.

Since it was such a big, late lunch, the family had warmed pie a la mode for a quick dinner and was in bed relatively early. Mom, especially, was already into a deep sleep as Daddy finished his prayers with the kids. His breathing quickened as he thought about the attic and the blood on the wall. His eyes gave off a cold, blue-green glare. He quietly went up the curved steps to the attic. As he gazed at the wall, the ruby writing glistened in the phosphorescent radiance of his eyes.

Grinning, he recalled the night he did it. It began in the calf barn, with a mangy, stray cat and a small white plastic ice cream pail . . . .

That truly was an auspicious night. Normally, Daddy didn't check the calf barn when doing his late chores, but this night, there was a show of power for what I wanted. As usual, Daddy went out the back screen door and walked across the lawn, only this time, he went into the well house and grabbed a little white pail, on his way to do the chores.

After finishing, he walked into the calf barn and locked all the doors, for I, Morbose, had already summoned a feral cat to be waiting in there. Daddy left the lights off, for evil can see in dark or light. Daddy caught chartreuse eyes, over in the far corner, aimed straight back at him. It hissed, showing the full length of fanged teeth. It snarled loudly, as it comprehended its unprotected soul was doomed, about to end in an agonizing death.

When Daddy, reached for the pitchfork, the creature whined. It glared fixedly at Daddy as it crept slowly along the back wall, caterwauling. Daddy eased along, until he was right up on the varmint, and then threw the pitchfork with all his might. Three prongs went straight through the whole cat, one into the head right through its eye and brain and the other two prongs into the cat's body.

The creature screeched in horrid pain as Daddy pulled it off the prongs, dropped the pitchfork and grabbed the small pail. Now, I wanted to see for myself how he held the cat's head back with one hand and used the other to hold its feet down. He clamped his teeth into the neck, pulling away lacerating the whole thing. Blood gushed out all over his hands, as he tried to hold it over the pail, not wanting to waste a trickle. He tried for every drop possible—he even bit into the unstaunched gaping neck wound again, ripping more flesh away and sending a new surge of blood into the filling pail, waiting below. After the last dribble was in the pail, he put the lid on it, took the corpse and threw it on top of the manure pile.

Daddy returned to the house and climbed the stairs to the attic. Once there, he closed the door, uncovered the pail, and dipped his fingers in its still warm contents. With a gleeful smile on his face, he began to finger paint the words.

When he was done, I admired my masterpiece through his eyes. After a few minutes of indulging myself, I had Daddy put the lid back on the bucket and leave it below the writing. I figured that no one would notice its disappearance, just as no one but me and Daddy would see my handiwork. Forgot of Aunt Linda.

Just then, Daddy recovered his lecherous self. He wanted Joe this very night. He did not want to remember writing on the wall with the fresh pail of cat's blood. He abruptly headed for the curved stairwell.

Daddy's member was already starting to get hard, as he walked over to Joe's moonlit, naked body. Rolling over to accommodate Daddy on the bed with him, Joe couldn't believe that Daddy had actually showed up to make love to him. This wasn't quite what Daddy had in mind, though. He was just horny and wanted to get off quickly and get his butt into bed with Mom, in case she woke up. I, meanwhile, wanted to experience what it's truly like to be with someone, before my time in this body was up.

Lying down next to Joe, I had Daddy turn over and give him a full, deep, wet kiss. It seemed to linger into endless bliss for Joe, who couldn't keep from moaning and groaning, for the untouched pleasures were too much for him. Daddy wrapped his big arms around Joe and pulled him under himself, more than ready to make passionate, hungry love to Joe, just as he wanted. Kissing Joe's neck softly, Daddy didn't stop there. He made love to Joe's chest with his big wet lips, caressing the nipples erect. Daddy wanted to push it right in, but Joe wouldn't let him. Joe put it between his legs, where he could feel the aroused, throbbing flesh, as it craved his burning hot desire.

Some really weird things were going on with Aunt Linda. Never in her whole life had she looked so horrific. A putrid feeling had overcome her whole being. All of her teeth were turning a dingy, gray color and her breath smelled foul, an abnormally raunchy odor. Yesterday, she lost an upper right front tooth when she was eating a bagel with cream cheese. It just broke off at the gum line. That bagel had been the first thing in a while that she'd been able to keep in her queasy stomach without getting sick all over again.

Nights for Linda were endless, with hallucinating nightmares as she tried to sleep, but could not. No sleep and grueling knife-stabbing cramps, with the loss of quite a lot of blood, put her into another realm of existence. Just to get a few winks, she would have to pop sleeping pills, one after the other. After she awoke, her world was even more bizarre than before.

I don't know how Rashma became a fetus or even lasted long enough to be born, because something wasn't right within Aunt Linda's womb. The profuse bleeding from her uterus that started after his conception didn't slow even a fraction, it only got much worse as time passed. Did he not know there was no turning back once one is inside the placenta? Now that he was a vampire inside of a human, he was almost powerless, inside of the water sack. (Vampires are literally paralyzed in water.) Did he not know Aunt Linda's infections were so numerous that when an ovum was deposited in her uterus, it never went beyond the embryo stage before she miscarried? Rashma, why in God's name have you done this?

Routine returned to the farm and before I knew it, the month changed. It was now December 1, in your year, 1962. Time for me to leave my father's body and transceive into my mother's womb. Under normal circumstances, this would produce a member of the same species. I held fast to the idea of energizing enough power to completely change Mom's female germ cell, so it would be exclusively mine to mold; a demonic, animate soul that could feel, smell and taste all the fruits of God's given, Mother Earth.

I worked overtime with Daddy. I wanted to make sure he spent lots of quality, foreplay time with Mom, to ensure the consummation would be a complete success. This meant another life for me, a brand-new beginning. It *had* to happen— I've been planning this for far too long, to have everything fall through.

It took some doing to get him to have the same wantonness he had with Joe. I made him do unreal things with his big fingers, which drove Mom into a state of ecstasy. She craved Daddy inside of her. This only multiplied his urges for the release of his infiltrating sperm into my mother's waiting womb. I wanted to make sure everything was right, not ever having done anything like this before. I made unquestioning moves to have every bit of my power ready to go in a split second's notice. It went better than I expected, a perfect conjugation.

Only seconds after Daddy entered the world of bliss, I said to myself, *NOW, Morbose, NOW, or forever hold yourself as a dark space.*

And if I perish, I perish.
Esther 4:16

The endless amount of sleeping pills Aunt Linda had taken finally caught up with her, as the clock chimed 2:00 A.M. Earlier, feeling fevered, she had fallen asleep on top of her puffy, white comforter. Exhausted by all that had transpired:

she was oblivious when her water sac broke, way too early, unleashing the baby's demonic power. Blood started to dribble out of her vagina as she half did a twisting lurch to her right side; still drugged, hoping that it was only a hideous nightmare.

Rashma pushed up her whole stomach area and abdomen, as he turned around, in a desperate effort to get out. Not only was he extremely premature, he didn't need to be stillborn on top of everything else . . . but if he was, he still might make it without being caught, if he prevailed at the grave site and moved on from there.

Asleep, Linda still squirmed, as the throes increased, rolling her torpid body back and forth. Her cervical opening wasn't dilated at all, making it very difficult for Rashma to get through. He was already completely free of his afterbirth as he scratched the uterine walls frantically and bit at the cervix, striving to get out, before the blood and fluids drowned him, exhausting and choking the very powers of what he wanted to be. Or was going to be.

It was his last-ditch endeavor to squeeze out onto the white comforter and quickly haul himself up into Aunt Linda's nightgown on the way to her neck, leaving a thick swath of fresh, steaming blood everywhere he went. He opened his grotesque mouth. Four razor sharp teeth slid out of his gums, an inch long. As the thing came closer to her neck to bite the jugular, his eyes blazed with an icy, hollow blue. He sank glistening teeth far into the pulsing vein. Making sucking noises and groaning at the taste of the lifeblood that was now his very existence, he started to go for the other side of Linda's neck, just as she partially woke up to the nightmare turned so real.

Screaming bloody murder, Linda reached for the phone beside the bed to call Bill. She was hysterical and before she could blurt out much to him, she passed out onto the blood-soaked bed, the phone falling to the floor, with a ringing crash.

In shocked horror, Daddy got dressed as fast as he could, grabbing the double-barreled shotgun on his way out the door. He drove eighty miles an hour and did not care if he got a ticket—he wasn't going to stop until he got there, for nothing in his life had ever scared him this bad. Not knowing what had Aunt Linda in such frantic distress, made him think all kinds of crazy things might have happened to her.

Daddy kicked in Aunt Linda's door to find her lying on the blood-drenched bed in shock with a pillow wrapped around her head as if she was trying to suffocate herself. He grabbed the pillow to pull it away as she screamed it was coming after her again. He didn't know what the hell was going on, so he told her to get dressed fast, and then he would take her to Nanna and Pappa Marbello's house.

Totally confused, he looked around and saw that Bushy Butt and Petrey's cage had been knocked over and the door was hanging wide open. Both lovebirds were missing. He turned to go back down the hallway to the bathroom where Aunt Linda was showering. As he returned to the bedroom, a trail of wet blood caught his eye. It was Rashma's blood, dripping off his still-wet, slimy body as he darted into the open closet.

Pausing by the closet, Daddy called to see if she was ready to go, yet. He told her to hurry, please, as she came out to get some clothes to take with her.

In the closet, Aunt Linda pushed her clothes aside. She shrieked and he yelled in holy terror as they both saw ugly, little Rashma with one of her birds in his malignant bite. He'd drained its blood, sucking every bit of life possible, until its poor, small heart collapsed.

Daddy took the safety off the shotgun, aimed and fired, hitting the fetid flesh square on and spattering it everywhere, in the upper shelf of the closet.

With a shrill scream, violent and wicked, Rashma jumped down. He scrambled and slid across the living room floor, toward the front door, as Daddy shot again, with his last bullet. Blood and flesh were all over the floor. A mangled Rashma escaped out the door, in what they thought was the direction of the woods. Aunt Linda made Daddy drag the scared to death Chan Chan, the white Maltese, out from under the bed and they flew out of there in the other direction to get away from this ghastly nightmare. On the way to the senior Marbellos' house, Daddy and Aunt Linda got their stories straight about what happened. To everyone else, they'd say she lost the baby from a miscarriage. Maybe now, she could get back into good health with some decent care and nurturing from Nanna and Pappa Marbello. Neither of them could speak of the gruesome thing they thought was left behind.

It was only the beginning of Rashma's deceptions:

He is a merchant, the balances of deceit are in his hand: he loveth to oppress.
Hosea 12:7

Lay heavy upon you!

A Twist of Fate

The Prana energies were too strong for me, I was like a Tiger stalking, taking in all. It was forcing me to ambush my own plans: like a starving phrenetic circling shark, going straight for the kill. I couldn't help myself.

Tis time now for all, I must tip thy soon to be twin brother's heel a bit to ensure my predestined place upon your earth. You will see!

God will give me magical powers just like it says in your Bible. POWER Magical POWER. He even puts it in writing.

God given also is Rashma whom in the future will literally feed himself to <u>fat hogs</u>.

Maybe, just maybe, I am NOT looking for power.

Thou Fool, this soul shall be
required of thee
St luke 12:30

COME: FOLLOW ME
FLY WITH ME, READ ME!